MUCH ADO ABOUT NOTHING

EDITED BY

TUCKER BROOKE

TABLE OF CONTENTS

The facsimile opposite represents the title-page of the Elizabethan Club copy of the only early quarto edition. Fifteen copies of this edition are known to survive.

Much adoe about Nothing

As it hath been sundrie times publikely
acted by the right honourable, the Lord
Chamberlaine his seruants.

Written by William Shakespeare.

LONDON
Printed by V.S. for Andrew Wise, and
William Aspley.
1600.

DRAMATIS PERSONÆ

DON PEDRO, *Prince of Arragon*

LEONATO, *Governor of Messina*

DON JOHN, *Bastard Brother to Don Pedro*

CLAUDIO, *a young Lord of Florence, Favourite to Don Pedro*

BENEDICK, *a young Lord of Padua, favour'd likewise by Don Pedro*

ANTONIO, *Brother to Leonato*

BALTHASAR, *Servant to Don Pedro*

BORACHIO, *Confidant to Don John*

CONRADE, *Friend to Borachio*

DOGBERRY, *a constable,*
VERGES, *a headborough,* } *two foolish Officers*

FRIAR FRANCIS

(INNOGEN, *Wife to Leonato*)

HERO, *Daughter to Leonato and Innogen*

BEATRICE, *Niece to Leonato*

MARGARET,
URSULA, } *two Gentlewomen attending on Hero*

A Sexton, a Boy in attendance on Benedick, Messengers, members of the Night Watch, and other Attendants

SCENE: *Messina in Sicily.*

Much Ado About Nothing

ACT FIRST

Scene One

[Before Antonio's Orchard]

Enter Leonato, Governor of Messina; Innogen, his wife; Hero, his daughter; and Beatrice, his niece; with a Messenger.

Leon. I learn in this letter that Don Pedro of Arragon comes this night to Messina.

Mess. He is very near by this: he was not three leagues off when I left him.

Leon. How many gentlemen have you lost in this action?

Mess. But few of any sort, and none of name.

Leon. A victory is twice itself when the achiever brings home full numbers. I find here that Don Pedro hath bestowed much honour on a young Florentine called Claudio.

Mess. Much deserved on his part and equally remembered by Don Pedro. He hath borne himself beyond the promise of his age, doing in the figure of a lamb the feats of a lion: he hath indeed better bettered expectation than you must expect of me to tell you how.

Leon. He hath an uncle here in Messina will be very much glad of it.

Mess. I have already delivered him letters, and there appears much joy in him; even so

7 sort: *rank; cf. n.* name: *reputation*

much that joy could not show itself modest enough without a badge of bitterness.

Leon. Did he break out into tears?

Mess. In great measure.

Leon. A kind overflow of kindness. There are no faces truer than those that are so washed: how much better is it to weep at joy than to joy at weeping!

Beat. I pray you is Signior Mountanto returned from the wars or no?

Mess. I know none of that name, lady: there was none such in the army of any sort.

Leon. What is he that you ask for, niece?

Hero. My cousin means Signior Benedick of Padua.

Mess. O! he is returned, and as pleasant as ever he was.

Beat. He set up his bills here in Messina and challenged Cupid at the flight; and my uncle's fool, reading the challenge, subscribed for Cupid, and challenged him at the bird-bolt. I pray you, how many hath he killed and eaten in these wars? But how many hath he killed? for, indeed, I promised to eat all of his killing.

Leon. Faith, niece, you tax Signior Benedick too much; but he'll be meet with you, I doubt it not.

Mess. He hath done good service, lady, in these wars.

Beat. You had musty victual, and he hath

23 badge: *distinguishing mark*
26 kind: *natural*
30 Mountanto; *cf. n.*
37 pleasant: *given to joking*
39 bills: *advertisement*
40 at the flight: *at long-distance archery*
41 subscribed: *signed*
42 bird-bolt: *blunt arrow for shooting birds; cf. n.*
46 tax: *blame*
47 meet with: *even with*

holp to eat it: he is a very valiant trencher-man; he hath an excellent stomach.

Mess. And a good soldier too, lady.

Beat. And a good soldier to a lady; but what is he to a lord?

Mess. A lord to a lord, a man to a man, stuffed with all honourable virtues.

Beat. It is so, indeed; he is no less than a stuffed man; but for the stuffing,—well, we are all mortal.

Leon. You must not, sir, mistake my niece. There is a kind of merry war betwixt Signior Benedick and her: they never meet but there's a skirmish of wit between them.

Beat. Alas! he gets nothing by that. In our last conflict four of his five wits went halting off, and now is the whole man governed with one! so that if he have wit enough to keep himself warm, let him bear it for a difference between himself and his horse; for it is all the wealth that he hath left to be known a reasonable creature. Who is his companion now? He hath every month a new sworn brother.

Mess. Is't possible?

Beat. Very easily possible: he wears his faith but as the fashion of his hat; it ever changes with the next block.

Mess. I see, lady, the gentleman is not in your books.

Beat. No; an he were, I would burn my

52 trencher-man: *glutton* 60 stuffed . . stuffing; *cf. n.*
67 five wits; *cf. n.* went halting off: *retired limping*
70 difference; *cf. n.* 72 to be known, *etc.*; *cf. n.*
76 faith: *fidelity* 78 next block: *newest fashion (hat-mould)*
80 books: '*good books*'

study. But, I pray you, who is his companion? Is there no young squarer now that will make a voyage with him to the devil?

Mess. He is most in the company of the right noble Claudio.

Beat. O Lord! he will hang upon him like a disease: he is sooner caught than the pestilence, and the taker runs presently mad. God help the noble Claudio! if he have caught the Benedick, it will cost him a thousand pound ere a' be cured.

Mess. I will hold friends with you, lady.

Beat. Do, good friend.

Leon. You will never run mad, niece.

Beat. No, not till a hot January.

Mess. Don Pedro is approached.

Enter Don Pedro, Claudio, Benedick, Balthazar, and John the Bastard.

D. Pedro. Good Signior Leonato, you are come to meet your trouble: the fashion of the world is to avoid cost, and you encounter it.

Leon. Never came trouble to my house in the likeness of your Grace, for trouble being gone, comfort should remain; but when you depart from me, sorrow abides and happiness takes his leave.

D. Pedro. You embrace your charge too willingly. I think this is your daughter.

Leon. Her mother hath many times told me so.

83 squarer: *quarreller* 89 presently: *immediately*
90 the Benedick; *cf. n.* 91 a': *he* 100 encounter: *go towards*
106 embrace your charge: *accept your burden*

Bene. Were you in doubt, sir, that you asked her?

Leon. Signior Benedick, no; for then you were a child.

D. Pedro. You have it full, Benedick: we may guess by this what you are, being a man. Truly, the lady fathers herself. Be happy, lady, for you are like an honourable father.

Bene. If Signior Leonato be her father, she would not have his head on her shoulders for all Messina, as like him as she is.

Beat. I wonder that you will still be talking, Signior Benedick: nobody marks you.

Bene. What! my dear Lady Disdain, are you yet living?

Beat. Is it possible Disdain should die while she hath such meet food to feed it as Signior Benedick? Courtesy itself must convert to disdain, if you come in her presence.

Bene. Then is courtesy a turncoat. But it is certain I am loved of all ladies, only you excepted; and I would I could find in my heart that I had not a hard heart; for, truly, I love none.

Beat. A dear happiness to women: they would else have been troubled with a pernicious suitor. I thank God and my cold blood, I am of your humour for that: I had rather hear my dog bark at a crow than a man swear he loves me.

Bene. God keep your ladyship still in that

114 full: *full in the face*
116 fathers herself: *shows who is her father*
121 still: *always* 126 meet: *proper* 127 convert: *change*
134 dear happiness: *rare luck* 137 humour: *disposition*

mind; so some gentleman or other shall 'scape a predestinate scratched face.

Beat. Scratching could not make it worse, an 'twere such a face as yours were.

Bene. Well, you are a rare parrot-teacher.

Beat. A bird of my tongue is better than a beast of yours.

Bene. I would my horse had the speed of your tongue, and so good a continuer. But keep your way, i' God's name; I have done.

Beat. You always end with a jade's trick: I know you of old.

D. Pedro. This is the sum of all, Leonato.—Signior Claudio, and Signior Benedick, my dear friend Leonato hath invited you all. I tell him we shall stay here at the least a month, and he heartily prays some occasion may detain us longer: I dare swear he is no hypocrite, but prays from his heart.

Leon. If you swear, my lord, you shall not be forsworn. [*To Don John.*] Let me bid you welcome, my lord: being reconciled to the prince your brother, I owe you all duty.

D. John. I thank you: I am not of many words, but I thank you.

Leon. Please it your Grace lead on?

D. Pedro. Your hand, Leonato; we will go together.

Exeunt all but Benedick and Claudio.

Claud. Benedick, didst thou note the daughter of Signior Leonato?

142 predestinate; *cf. n.* 143 an: *if; cf. n.* 146 bird, *etc.; cf. n.*
149 so good a continuer: *equal staying powers*
151 jade's trick; *cf. n.* 162 being: *since you are*

Bene. I noted her not; but I looked on her.

Claud. Is she not a modest young lady?

Bene. Do you question me, as an honest man should do, for my simple true judgment; or would you have me speak after my custom, as being a professed tyrant to their sex?

Claud. No; I pray thee speak in sober judgment.

Bene. Why, i' faith, methinks she's too low for a high praise, too brown for a fair praise, and too little for a great praise: only this commendation I can afford her, that were she other than she is, she were unhandsome, and being no other but as she is, I do not like her.

Claud. Thou thinkest I am in sport: I pray thee tell me truly how thou likest her.

Bene. Would you buy her, that you inquire after her?

Claud. Can the world buy such a jewel?

Bene. Yea, and a case to put it into. But speak you this with a sad brow, or do you play the flouting Jack, to tell us Cupid is a good hare-finder, and Vulcan a rare carpenter? Come, in what key shall a man take you, to go in the song?

Claud. In mine eye she is the sweetest lady that ever I looked on.

Bene. I can see yet without spectacles and I see no such matter: there's her cousin an she were not possessed with a fury, exceeds her as much in beauty as the first of May doth the last

171 noted; *cf. n.*
176 tyrant: *fault-finder*
191 sad: *serious*
192 flouting Jack: *mocking fellow*
192 Cupid, *etc.; cf. n.*
194 go in: *join in*

of December. But I hope you have no intent to turn husband, have you?

Claud. I would scarce trust myself, though I had sworn to the contrary, if Hero would be my wife.

Bene. Is't come to this, i' faith? Hath not the world one man but he will wear his cap with suspicion? Shall I never see a bachelor of three-score again? Go to, i' faith; an thou wilt needs thrust thy neck into a yoke, wear the print of it, and sigh away Sundays. Look! Don Pedro is returned to seek you.

Enter Don Pedro.

D. Pedro. What secret hath held you here, that you followed not to Leonato's?

Bene. I would your Grace would constrain me to tell.

D. Pedro. I charge thee on thy allegiance.

Bene. You hear, Count Claudio: I can be secret as a dumb man; I would have you think so; but on my allegiance, mark you this, on my allegiance: he is in love. With who? now that is your Grace's part. Mark how short his answer is: with Hero, Leonato's short daughter.

Claud. If this were so, so were it uttered.

Bene. Like the old tale, my lord: 'it is not so, nor 'twas not so; but, indeed, God forbid it should be so.'

Claud. If my passion change not shortly, God forbid it should be otherwise.

208 wear his cap, *etc.*; *cf. n.*
210 Go to: *come!*
212 sigh away Sundays; *cf. n.*
226 the old tale; *cf. n.*

D. Pedro. Amen, if you love her; for the lady is very well worthy.

Claud. You speak this to fetch me in, my lord.

D. Pedro. By my troth, I speak my thought.

Claud. And in faith, my lord, I spoke mine.

Bene. And by my two faiths and troths, my lord, I spoke mine.

Claud. That I love her, I feel.

D. Pedro. That she is worthy, I know.

Bene. That I neither feel how she should be loved nor know how she should be worthy, is the opinion that fire cannot melt out of me: I will die in it at the stake.

D. Pedro. Thou wast ever an obstinate heretic in the despite of beauty.

Claud. And never could maintain his part but in the force of his will.

Bene. That a woman conceived me, I thank her; that she brought me up, I likewise give her most humble thanks: but that I will have a recheat winded in my forehead, or hang my bugle in an invisible baldrick, all women shall pardon me. Because I will not do them the wrong to mistrust any, I will do myself the right to trust none; and the fine is,—for the which I may go the finer,—I will live a bachelor.

D. Pedro. I shall see thee, ere I die, look pale with love.

Bene. With anger, with sickness, or with hunger, my lord; not with love: prove that ever I lose more blood with love than I will get again with drinking, pick out mine eyes with a ballad-

233 fetch . . in: *entrap*
245 despite: *contempt*
251 recheat, *etc.*; *cf. n.*
255 fine: *end*
256 go the finer: *wear finer clothes*
260 prove: *if you discover*

maker's pen, and hang me up at the door of a brothel-house for the sign of blind Cupid.

D. Pedro. Well, if ever thou dost fall from this faith, thou wilt prove a notable argument.

Bene. If I do, hang me in a bottle like a cat and shoot at me; and he that hits me, let him be clapped on the shoulder, and called Adam.

D. Pedro. Well, as time shall try:
'In time the savage bull doth bear the yoke.'

Bene. The savage bull may; but if ever the sensible Benedick bear it, pluck off the bull's horns and set them in my forehead; and let me be vilely painted, and in such great letters as they write, 'Here is good horse to hire,' let them signify under my sign 'Here you may see Benedick the married man.'

Claud. If this should ever happen, thou wouldst be horn-mad.

D. Pedro. Nay, if Cupid have not spent all his quiver in Venice, thou wilt quake for this shortly.

Bene. I look for an earthquake too then.

D. Pedro. Well, you will temporize with the hours. In the meantime, good Signior Benedick, repair to Leonato's: commend me to him and tell him I will not fail him at supper; for indeed he hath made great preparation.

Bene. I have almost matter enough in me for such an embassage; and so I commit you—

Claud. To the tuition of God: from my house, if I had it,—

264 sign . . Cupid; *cf. n.* 266 argument: *theme for talk*
267 bottle; *cf. n.* 269 Adam; *cf. n.* 270 try: *prove*
271 *Cf. n.* 280 horn-mad: *mad as a horned beast*
282 Venice; *cf. n.* 284 temporize; *cf. n.*
291 tuition: *protection; cf. n.*

D. Pedro. The sixth of July: your loving friend, Benedick.

Bene. Nay, mock not, mock not. The body of your discourse is sometime guarded with fragments, and the guards are but slightly basted on neither: ere you flout old ends any further, examine your conscience: and so I leave you.

Exit.

Claud. My liege, your highness now may do me good.

D. Pedro. My love is thine to teach: teach it but how,
And thou shalt see how apt it is to learn
Any hard lesson that may do thee good.

Claud. Hath Leonato any son, my lord?

D. Pedro. No child but Hero; she's his only heir.
Dost thou affect her, Claudio?

Claud. O! my lord,
When you went onward on this ended action,
I looked upon her with a soldier's eye,
That lik'd, but had a rougher task in hand
Than to drive liking to the name of love;
But now I am return'd, and that war-thoughts
Have left their places vacant, in their rooms
Come thronging soft and delicate desires,
All prompting me how fair young Hero is,
Saying, I lik'd her ere I went to wars.

D. Pedro. Thou wilt be like a lover presently,
And tire the hearer with a book of words.
If thou dost love fair Hero, cherish it,
And I will break with her, and with her father,

296 guarded: *trimmed; cf. n.* 297 guards: *trimmings*
306 affect: *love* 319 break: *open negotiations*

And thou shalt have her. Was't not to this end
That thou began'st to twist so fine a story?
Claud. How sweetly do you minister to love,
That know love's grief by his complexion!
But lest my liking might too sudden seem,
I would have salv'd it with a longer treatise.
D. Pedro. What need the bridge much broader than the flood?
The fairest grant is the necessity.
Look, what will serve is fit: 'tis once, thou lov'st,
And I will fit thee with the remedy.
I know we shall have revelling to-night:
I will assume thy part in some disguise,
And tell fair Hero I am Claudio;
And in her bosom I'll unclasp my heart,
And take her hearing prisoner with the force
And strong encounter of my amorous tale:
Then, after to her father will I break;
And the conclusion is, she shall be thine.
In practice let us put it presently. *Exeunt.*

Scene Two

[*Leonato's House*]

Enter Leonato and [*Antonio,*] *an old man, brother to Leonato.*

Leon. How now, brother! Where is my cousin, your son? Hath he provided this music?

Ant. He is very busy about it. But, brother, I can tell you strange news that you yet dreamt not of.

321 twist: *spin* 323 complexion: *outward appearance*
325 salv'd: *softened* 327 *Cf. n.* 328 'tis once: *once for all*
2 cousin: *nephew; cf. n.*

Leon. Are they good?

Ant. As the event stamps them: but they have a good cover; they show well outward. The prince and Count Claudio, walking in a thick-pleached alley in my orchard, were thus much overheard by a man of mine: the prince discovered to Claudio that he loved my niece your daughter, and meant to acknowledge it this night in a dance; and, if he found her accordant, he meant to take the present time by the top and instantly break with you of it.

Leon. Hath the fellow any wit that told you this?

Ant. A good sharp fellow: I will send for him; and question him yourself.

Leon. No, no; we will hold it as a dream till it appear itself: but I will acquaint my daughter withal, that she may be the better prepared for an answer, if peradventure this be true. Go you, and tell her of it. [*Several persons cross the stage.*] Cousins, you know what you have to do. O! I cry you mercy, friend; go you with me, and I will use your skill. Good cousin, have a care this busy time. *Exeunt.*

8 event: *outcome*
11 thick-pleached: *hedged with intertwining branches*
13 discovered: *revealed*
16 accordant: *consenting*
17 top: *forelock*
23 appear: *make evident*
24 withal: *therewith*
28 cry you mercy: *beg pardon*

Scene Three

[*The Same*]

Enter Sir John the Bastard and Conrade, his companion.

Con. What the good-year, my lord! why are you thus out of measure sad?

D. John. There is no measure in the occasion that breeds; therefore the sadness is without limit.

Con. You should hear reason.

D. John. And when I have heard it, what blessing brings it?

Con. If not a present remedy, at least a patient sufferance.

D. John. I wonder that thou, being,—as thou say'st thou art,—born under Saturn, goest about to apply a moral medicine to a mortifying mischief. I cannot hide what I am: I must be sad when I have cause, and smile at no man's jests; eat when I have stomach, and wait for no man's leisure; sleep when I am drowsy, and tend on no man's business; laugh when I am merry, and claw no man in his humour.

Con. Yea; but you must not make the full show of this till you may do it without controlment. You have of late stood out against your brother, and he hath ta'en you newly into his grace; where it is impossible you should take

1 good-year: *an unexplained expletive*
2 out of measure: *immeasurably*
12 born under Saturn; *cf. n.*
13 mortifying mischief: *deadly disease*
17 tend on: *attend to*
19 claw: *tickle, flatter*

true root but by the fair weather that you make yourself: it is needful that you frame the season for your own harvest.

D. John. I had rather be a canker in a hedge than a rose in his grace; and it better fits my blood to be disdained of all than to fashion a carriage to rob love from any: in this, though I cannot be said to be a flattering honest man, it must not be denied but I am a plain-dealing villain. I am trusted with a muzzle and enfranchised with a clog; therefore I have decreed not to sing in my cage. If I had my mouth, I would bite; if I had my liberty, I would do my liking: in the meantime, let me be that I am, and seek not to alter me.

Con. Can you make no use of your discontent?

D. John. I make all use of it, for I use it only. Who comes here?

Enter Borachio.

What news, Borachio?

Bora. I came yonder from a great supper: the prince, your brother, is royally entertained by Leonato; and I can give you intelligence of an intended marriage.

D. John. Will it serve for any model to build mischief on? What is he for a fool that betroths himself to unquietness?

Bora. Marry, it is your brother's right hand.

D. John. Who? the most exquisite Claudio?

Bora. Even he.

26 frame: *produce* 28 canker: *dog-rose*
30 blood: *temper* fashion a carriage: *counterfeit a behavior*
35 enfranchised: *liberated* 49 What . . for: *What kind of*

D. John. A proper squire! And who, and who? which way looks he?

Bora. Marry, on Hero, the daughter and heir of Leonato.

D. John. A very forward March-chick! How came you to this?

Bora. Being entertained for a perfumer, as I was smoking a musty room, comes me the prince and Claudio, hand in hand, in sad conference: I whipt me behind the arras, and there heard it agreed upon that the prince should woo Hero for himself, and having obtained her, give her to Count Claudio.

D. John. Come, come; let us thither: this may prove food to my displeasure. That young start-up hath all the glory of my overthrow: if I can cross him any way, I bless myself every way. You are both sure, and will assist me?

Bora. } *Con.* } To the death, my lord.

D. John. Let us to the great supper: their cheer is the greater that I am subdued. Would the cook were of my mind! Shall we go prove what's to be done?

Bora. We'll wait upon your lordship. *Exeunt.*

54 proper: *fine* 58 March-chick: *prematurely hatched chicken*
60 entertained: *employed* 61 smoking, *etc.; cf. n.*
69 start-up: *upstart* 71 sure: *trustworthy*

ACT SECOND

Scene One

[*A Hall in Leonato's House*]

Enter Leonato; [*Antonio,*] *his brother; his wife; Hero, his daughter; and Beatrice, his niece; and a kinsman.*

Leon. Was not Count John here at supper?

Ant. I saw him not.

Beat. How tartly that gentleman looks! I never can see him but I am heart-burned an hour after.

Hero. He is of a very melancholy disposition.

Beat. He were an excellent man that were made just in the mid-way between him and Benedick: the one is too like an image, and says nothing; and the other too like my lady's eldest son, evermore tattling.

Leon. Then half Signior Benedick's tongue in Count John's mouth, and half Count John's melancholy in Signior Benedick's face,—

Beat. With a good leg and a good foot, uncle, and money enough in his purse, such a man would win any woman in the world, if a' could get her good will.

Leon. By my troth, niece, thou wilt never get thee a husband, if thou be so shrewd of thy tongue.

Ant. In faith, she's too curst.

Beat. Too curst is more than curst: I shall lessen God's sending that way; for it is said,

4 heart-burned: *dyspeptic*
20 shrewd: *sharp*
22 curst: *ill-tempered*

'God sends a curst cow short horns;' but to a cow too curst he sends none.

Leon. So, by being too curst, God will send you no horns?

Beat. Just, if he send me no husband; for the which blessing I am at him upon my knees every morning and evening. Lord! I could not endure a husband with a beard on his face: I had rather lie in the woollen.

Leon. You may light on a husband that hath no beard.

Beat. What should I do with him? dress him in my apparel and make him my waiting-gentlewoman? He that hath a beard is more than a youth, and he that hath no beard is less than a man; and he that is more than a youth is not for me; and he that is less than a man, I am not for him: therefore I will even take sixpence in earnest of the bear-ward, and lead his apes into hell.

Leon. Well then, go you into hell?

Beat. No; but to the gate; and there will the devil meet me, like an old cuckold, with horns on his head, and say, 'Get you to heaven, Beatrice, get you to heaven; here's no place for you maids:' so deliver I up my apes, and away to Saint Peter for the heavens; he shows me where the bachelors sit, and there live we as merry as the day is long.

Ant. [*To Hero.*] Well, niece, I trust you will be ruled by your father.

29 Just: *just so*
33 lie in the woollen: *sleep between blankets (without sheets)*
43 earnest: *advance wages* bear-ward: *trainer of bears (and often apes)* lead . . hell; *cf. n.*
47 cuckold: *deceived husband* 51 for the heavens; *cf. n.*

Beat. Yes, faith; it is my cousin's duty to make curtsy, and say, 'Father, as it please you:' —but yet for all that, cousin, let him be a handsome fellow, or else make another curtsy, and say, 'Father, as it please me.'

Leon. Well, niece, I hope to see you one day fitted with a husband.

Beat. Not till God make men of some other metal than earth. Would it not grieve a woman to be over-mastered with a piece of valiant dust? to make an account of her life to a clod of wayward marl? No, uncle, I'll none: Adam's sons are my brethren; and truly, I hold it a sin to match in my kindred.

Leon. Daughter, remember what I told you: if the prince do solicit you in that kind, you know your answer.

Beat. The fault will be in the music, cousin, if you be not wooed in good time: if the prince be too important, tell him there is measure in everything, and so dance out the answer. For, hear me, Hero: wooing, wedding, and repenting, is as a Scotch jig, a measure, and a cinque-pace: the first suit is hot and hasty, like a Scotch jig, and full as fantastical; the wedding, mannerly-modest, as a measure, full of state and ancientry; and then comes Repentance, and, with his bad legs, falls into the cinque-pace faster and faster, till he sink into his grave.

Leon. Cousin, you apprehend passing shrewdly.

64 metal: *substance* 65 over-mastered with: *subject to*
67 marl: *clay* 75 important: *importunate*
78 measure: *a stately dance* cinque-pace: *lively dance*
80 mannerly-: *becomingly* 81 ancientry: *antique style*
85 apprehend: *understand* passing: *exceedingly*

Beat. I have a good eye, uncle: I can see a church by daylight.

Leon. The revellers are entering, brother: make good room. 89

Enter Prince Pedro, Claudio, Benedick, Balthazar, Don John, [Borachio, Margaret, Ursula, and other] Maskers with a drum.

D. Pedro. Lady, will you walk about with your friend?

Hero. So you walk softly and look sweetly and say nothing, I am yours for the walk; and especially when I walk away.

D. Pedro. With me in your company?

Hero. I may say so, when I please. 96

D. Pedro. And when please you to say so?

Hero. When I like your favour; for God defend the lute should be like the case!

D. Pedro. My visor is Philemon's roof; within the house is Jove. 101

Hero. Why, then, your visor should be thatch'd.

D. Pedro. Speak low, if you speak love. 104 [*Takes her aside.*]

Balth. Well, I would you did like me.

Marg. So would not I, for your own sake: for I have many ill qualities.

Balth. Which is one? 108

Marg. I say my prayers aloud.

Balth. I love you the better; the hearers may cry Amen.

Marg. God match me with a good dancer!

86 see a church; *cf. n.* 98 favour: *face* 99 defend: *forbid*
100 visor: *mask* Philemon's roof; *cf. n.* 107 ill: *bad*

Balth. Amen.

Marg. And God keep him out of my sight when the dance is done! Answer, clerk.

Balth. No more words: the clerk is answered.

Urs. I know you well enough: you are Signior Antonio.

Ant. At a word, I am not.

Urs. I know you by the waggling of your head.

Ant. To tell you true, I counterfeit him.

Urs. You could never do him so ill-well, unless you were the very man. Here's his dry hand up and down: you are he, you are he.

Ant. At a word, I am not.

Urs. Come, come; do you think I do not know you by your excellent wit? Can virtue hide itself? Go to, mum, you are he: graces will appear, and there's an end.

Beat. Will you not tell me who told you so?

Bene. No, you shall pardon me.

Beat. Nor will you not tell me who you are?

Bene. Not now.

Beat. That I was disdainful, and that I had my good wit out of the 'Hundred Merry Tales.' Well, this was Signior Benedick that said so.

Bene. What's he?

Beat. I am sure you know him well enough.

Bene. Not I, believe me.

Beat. Did he never make you laugh?

115 Answer, clerk; *cf. n.* 120 at a word: *to be brief*
124 do him so ill-well: *represent his imperfection so perfectly*
126 up and down: *all over* 131 an end: *no more to be said*
137 'Hundred Merry Tales'; *cf. n.*

Bene. I pray you, what is he?

Beat. Why, he is the prince's jester: a very dull fool; only his gift is in devising impossible slanders: none but libertines delight in him; and the commendation is not in his wit, but in his villainy; for he both pleases men and angers them, and then they laugh at him and beat him. I am sure he is in the fleet: I would he had boarded me!

Bene. When I know the gentleman, I'll tell him what you say.

Beat. Do, do: he'll but break a comparison or two on me; which, peradventure not marked or not laughed at, strikes him into melancholy; and then there's a partridge wing saved, for the fool will eat no supper that night. We must follow the leaders. *Music for the dance.*

Bene. In every good thing.

Beat. Nay, if they lead to any ill, I will leave them at the next turning. *Dance.*

Exeunt [all but Don John, Borachio, and Claudio].

D. John. Sure my brother is amorous on Hero, and hath withdrawn her father to break with him about it. The ladies follow her and but one visor remains.

Bora. And that is Claudio: I know him by his bearing.

D. John. Are you not Signior Benedick?

Claud. You know me well; I am he.

D. John. Signior, you are very near my

145 only his gift: *his only talent* 150 fleet; *cf. n.*
154 break a comparison: *crack a joke* 171 near: *intimate with*

brother in his love: he is enamoured on Hero; I pray you, dissuade him from her; she is no equal for his birth: you may do the part of an honest man in it.

Claud. How know you he loves her?

D. John. I heard him swear his affection.

Bora. So did I too; and he swore he would marry her to-night.

D. John. Come, let us to the banquet.

Exeunt Don John and Borachio.

Claud. Thus answer I in name of Benedick,
But hear these ill news with the ears of Claudio.
'Tis certain so; the prince woos for himself.
Friendship is constant in all other things
Save in the office and affairs of love:
Therefore all hearts in love use their own tongues;
Let every eye negotiate for itself
And trust no agent; for beauty is a witch
Against whose charms faith melteth into blood.
This is an accident of hourly proof,
Which I mistrusted not. Farewell, therefore, Hero!

Enter Benedick.

Bene. Count Claudio?

Claud. Yea, the same.

Bene. Come, will you go with me?

Claud. Whither?

Bene. Even to the next willow, about your own business, count. What fashion will you wear the garland of? About your neck, like a

183 certain: *certainly* 186 use; *cf. n.*
189 Against: *in contact with* 196 willow; *cf. n.*

usurer's chain? or under your arm, like a lieutenant's scarf? You must wear it one way, for the prince hath got your Hero. 201

Claud. I wish him joy of her.

Bene. Why, that's spoken like an honest drovier: so they sell bullocks. But did you think the prince would have served you thus? 205

Claud. I pray you, leave me.

Bene. Ho! now you strike like the blind man: 'twas the boy that stole your meat, and you'll beat the post. 209

Claud. If it will not be, I'll leave you. *Exit.*

Bene. Alas! poor hurt fowl. Now will he creep into sedges. But, that my lady Beatrice should know me, and not know me! The prince's fool! Ha! it may be I go under that title because I am merry. Yea, but so I am apt to do myself wrong; I am not so reputed: it is the base though bitter disposition of Beatrice that puts the world into her person, and so gives me out. Well, I'll be revenged as I may. 219

Enter the Prince.

D. Pedro. Now, signior, where's the count? Did you see him?

Bene. Troth, my lord, I have played the part of Lady Fame. I found him here as melancholy as a lodge in a warren. I told him, and I think I told him true, that your Grace had got the good will of this young lady; and I offered him

204 drovier: *cattle-dealer* 207 like the blind man; *cf. n.*
212 creep into sedges; *cf. n.* 217 base though bitter; *cf. n.*
218 puts . . person: *identifies the world with herself* gives me out: *represents me*
223 Lady Fame; *cf. n.*
224 lodge in a warren: *solitary game-keeper's hut*

my company to a willow tree, either to make
him a garland, as being forsaken, or to bind him
up a rod, as being worthy to be whipped. 229

D. Pedro. To be whipped! What's his fault?

Bene. The flat transgression of a school-boy,
who, being overjoy'd with finding a bird's nest,
shows it his companion, and he steals it. 233

D. Pedro. Wilt thou make a trust a transgression? The transgression is in the stealer.

Bene. Yet it had not been amiss the rod had
been made, and the garland too; for the garland
he might have worn himself, and the rod he
might have bestowed on you, who, as I take it,
have stolen his bird's nest. 240

D. Pedro. I will but teach them to sing, and restore them to the owner.

Bene. If their singing answer your saying, by
my faith, you say honestly. 244

D. Pedro. The Lady Beatrice hath a quarrel to you: the gentleman that danced with her told her she is much wronged by you.

Bene. O! she misused me past the endurance of a block: an oak but with one green leaf on it, would have answered her: my very visor began to assume life and scold with her. She told me, not thinking I had been myself, that I was the prince's jester; that I was duller than a great thaw; huddling jest upon jest with such impossible conveyance upon me, that I stood like a man at a mark, with a whole army shooting at

228 bind . . rod: *tie several willow switches into a scourge*
231 flat: *downright* 241 them: *the birds in the nest*
243, 244 *Cf. n.* 248 misused: *abused*
254 thaw: *unseasonable wet spell in winter* huddling: *piling*
255 impossible conveyance: *incredible jugglery*
256 man at a mark; *cf. n.*

me. She speaks poniards, and every word stabs: if her breath were as terrible as her terminations, there were no living near her; she would infect to the north star. I would not marry her, though she were endowed with all that Adam had left him before he transgressed: she would have made Hercules have turned spit, yea, and have cleft his club to make the fire too. Come, talk not of her; you shall find her the infernal Ate in good apparel. I would to God some scholar would conjure her, for certainly, while she is here, a man may live as quiet in hell as in a sanctuary; and people sin upon purpose because they would go thither; so, indeed, all disquiet, horror and perturbation follow her. 271

Enter Claudio, Beatrice, Hero, and Leonato.

D. Pedro. Look! here she comes.

Bene. Will your Grace command me any service to the world's end? I will go on the slightest errand now to the Antipodes that you can devise to send me on; I will fetch you a toothpicker now from the furthest inch of Asia; bring you the length of Prester John's foot; fetch you a hair off the Great Cham's beard; do you any embassage to the Pigmies, rather than hold three words' conference with this harpy. You have no employment for me? 282

D. Pedro. None, but to desire your good company.

258 terminations: *epithets* 259 infect, *etc.; cf. n.*
263 Hercules, *etc.; cf. n.* 265 infernal Ate, *etc.; cf. n.*
266 some scholar, *etc.; cf. n.*
278-282 Prester John's foot, *etc.; cf. notes*

Bene. O God, sir, here's a dish I love not: I cannot endure my Lady Tongue. *Exit.*

D. Pedro. Come, lady, come; you have lost the heart of Signior Benedick.

Beat. Indeed, my lord, he lent it me awhile; and I gave him use for it, a double heart for a single one: marry, once before he won it of me with false dice, therefore your Grace may well say I have lost it.

D. Pedro. You have put him down, lady, you have put him down.

Beat. So I would not he should do me, my lord, lest I should prove the mother of fools. I have brought Count Claudio, whom you sent me to seek.

D. Pedro. Why, how now, count! wherefore are you sad?

Claud. Not sad, my lord.

D. Pedro. How then? Sick?

Count. Neither, my lord.

Beat. The count is neither sad, nor sick, nor merry, nor well; but civil count, civil as an orange, and something of that jealous complexion.

D. Pedro. I' faith, lady, I think your blazon to be true; though, I'll be sworn, if he be so, his conceit is false. Here, Claudio, I have wooed in thy name, and fair Hero is won; I have broke with her father, and, his good will obtained; name the day of marriage, and God give thee joy!

Leon. Count, take of me my daughter, and

290 use: *usury, interest*
294 put him down: *vanquished him*
306 civil . . civil; *cf. n.*
309 blazon: *description*
311 conceit: *conception*

with her my fortunes: his Grace hath made the match, and all grace say Amen to it!

Beat. Speak, count, 'tis your cue.

Claud. Silence is the perfectest herald of joy: I were but little happy, if I could say how much. Lady, as you are mine, I am yours: I give away myself for you and dote upon the exchange.

Beat. Speak, cousin; or, if you cannot, stop his mouth with a kiss, and let not him speak neither.

D. Pedro. In faith, lady, you have a merry heart.

Beat. Yea, my lord; I thank it, poor fool, it keeps on the windy side of care. My cousin tells him in his ear that he is in her heart.

Claud. And so she doth, cousin.

Beat. Good Lord, for alliance! Thus goes every one to the world but I, and I am sun-burnt. I may sit in a corner and cry heigh-ho for a husband!

D. Pedro. Lady Beatrice, I will get you one.

Beat. I would rather have one of your father's getting. Hath your Grace ne'er a brother like you? Your father got excellent husbands, if a maid could come by them.

D. Pedro. Will you have me, lady?

Beat. No, my lord, unless I might have another for working days: your Grace is too costly to wear every day. But, I beseech your Grace, pardon me; I was born to speak all mirth and no matter.

317 all grace: *i.e. the grace of God*
329 windy: *windward (or advantageous)* tells . . ear: *whispers*
332 alliance; *cf. n.* goes . . to the world: *marries*
334 sun-burnt; *cf. n.* 338 getting: *begetting*
346 matter: *sense*

D. Pedro. Your silence most offends me, and to be merry best becomes you; for, out of question, you were born in a merry hour.

Beat. No, sure, my lord, my mother cried; but then there was a star danced, and under that was I born. Cousins, God give you joy! 352

Leon. Niece, will you look to those things I told you of?

Beat. I cry you mercy, uncle. By your Grace's pardon. *Exit Beatrice.*

D. Pedro. By my troth, a pleasant-spirited lady. 358

Leon. There's little of the melancholy element in her, my lord: she is never sad but when she sleeps; and not ever sad then, for I have heard my daughter say, she hath often dreamed of unhappiness and waked herself with laughing.

D. Pedro. She cannot endure to hear tell of a husband. 365

Leon. O! by no means: she mocks all her wooers out of suit.

D. Pedro. She were an excellent wife for Benedick. 369

Leon. O Lord! my lord, if they were but a week married, they would talk themselves mad.

D. Pedro. Count Claudio, when mean you to go to church? 373

Claud. To-morrow, my lord. Time goes on crutches till love have all his rites.

Leon. Not till Monday, my dear son, which is hence a just seven-night; and a time too brief too, to have all things answer my mind. 378

361 ever: *always* 367 suit: *courtship* 373 go to church: *marry*
378 answer my mind: *correspond with my intention*

D. Pedro. Come, you shake the head at so long a breathing; but, I warrant thee, Claudio, the time shall not go dully by us. I will in the interim undertake one of Hercules' labours, which is, to bring Signior Benedick and the Lady Beatrice into a mountain of affection the one with the other. I would fain have it a match; and I doubt not but to fashion it, if you three will but minister such assistance as I shall give you direction.

Leon. My lord, I am for you, though it cost me ten nights' watchings.

Claud. And I, my lord.

D. Pedro. And you too, gentle Hero?

Hero. I will do any modest office, my lord, to help my cousin to a good husband.

D. Pedro. And Benedick is not the unhopefullest husband that I know. Thus far can I praise him; he is of a noble strain, of approved valour, and confirmed honesty. I will teach you how to humour your cousin, that she shall fall in love with Benedick; and I, with your two helps, will so practise on Benedick that, in despite of his quick wit and his queasy stomach, he shall fall in love with Beatrice. If we can do this, Cupid is no longer an archer: his glory shall be ours, for we are the only love-gods. Go in with me, and I will tell you my drift.

Exeunt.

380 breathing: *delay*
387 minister: *offer*
389 am for you: *accept your proposal*
397 strain: *lineage* approved: *tested*
398 honesty: *honor*
402 queasy stomach: *squeamish taste*
406 drift: *purpose*

Scene Two

[*The Same*]

Enter Don John and Borachio.

D. John. It is so; the Count Claudio shall marry the daughter of Leonato.

Bora. Yea, my lord; but I can cross it.

D. John. Any bar, any cross, any impediment will be medicinable to me: I am sick in displeasure to him, and whatsoever comes athwart his affection ranges evenly with mine. How canst thou cross this marriage?

Bora. Not honestly, my lord; but so covertly that no dishonesty shall appear in me.

D. John. Show me briefly how.

Bora. I think I told your lordship, a year since, how much I am in the favour of Margaret, the waiting-gentlewoman to Hero.

D. John. I remember.

Bora. I can, at any unseasonable instant of the night, appoint her to look out at her lady's chamber-window.

D. John. What life is in that, to be the death of this marriage?

Bora. The poison of that lies in you to temper. Go you to the prince your brother; spare not to tell him, that he hath wronged his honour in marrying the renowned Claudio,—whose estimation do you mightily hold up,—to a contaminated stale, such a one as Hero.

D. John. What proof shall I make of that?

1 shall: *is to* 6 displeasure: *dislike*
7 affection: *liking* ranges evenly: *runs parallel*
21 lies in: *depends upon* 22 temper: *mix*
25 estimation: *worth* 26 stale: *wanton*

Bora. Proof enough to misuse the prince, to vex Claudio, to undo Hero, and kill Leonato. Look you for any other issue?

D. John. Only to despite them, I will endeavour any thing.

Bora. Go, then; find me a meet hour to draw Don Pedro and the Count Claudio alone: tell them that you know that Hero loves me; intend a kind of zeal both to the prince and Claudio, as—in love of your brother's honour, who hath made this match, and his friend's reputation, who is thus like to be cozened with the semblance of a maid,—that you have discovered thus. They will scarcely believe this without trial: offer them instances, which shall bear no less likelihood than to see me at her chamber-window, hear me call Margaret Hero; hear Margaret term me Claudio; and bring them to see this the very night before the intended wedding: for in the meantime I will so fashion the matter that Hero shall be absent; and there shall appear such seeming truth of Hero's disloyalty, that jealousy shall be called assurance, and all the preparation overthrown.

D. John. Grow this to what adverse issue it can, I will put it in practice. Be cunning in the working this, and thy fee is a thousand ducats.

Bora. Be you constant in the accusation, and my cunning shall not shame me.

D. John. I will presently go learn their day of marriage. *Exeunt.*

28 misuse: *delude* 35 intend: *pretend* 39 cozened: *deceived*
42 instances: *proofs* 45 term me Claudio; *cf. n.*
50 jealousy: *suspicion* 51 preparation: *i.e. for the marriage*
54 ducats: *Italian coins, worth about a dollar*

Scene Three

[*Leonato's Orchard*]

Enter Benedick, alone.

Bene. Boy!

[*Enter Boy.*]

Boy. Signior?

Bene. In my chamber-window lies a book; bring it hither to me in the orchard.

Boy. I am here already, sir.

Bene. I know that; but I would have thee hence, and here again. [*Exit Boy.*] I do much wonder that one man, seeing how much another man is a fool when he dedicates his behaviours to love, will, after he hath laughed at such shallow follies in others, become the argument of his own scorn by falling in love: and such a man is Claudio. I have known, when there was no music with him but the drum and the fife; and now had he rather hear the tabor and the pipe: I have known, when he would have walked ten mile afoot to see a good armour; and now will he lie ten nights awake, carving the fashion of a new doublet. He was wont to speak plain and to the purpose, like an honest man and a soldier; and now is he turned orthographer; his words are a very fantastical banquet, just so many strange dishes. May I be so converted, and see with these eyes? I cannot tell; I think not: I will not be sworn but love may transform me to an oyster; but I'll take my oath on it, till he

5 here already; *cf. n.* 15 tabor; *cf. n.* 18 carving: *moulding*
19 doublet: *close fitting coat*

have made an oyster of me, he shall never make me such a fool. One woman is fair, yet I am well; another is wise, yet I am well; another virtuous, yet I am well; but till all graces be in one woman, one woman shall not come in my grace. Rich she shall be, that's certain; wise, or I'll none; virtuous, or I'll never cheapen her; fair, or I'll never look on her; mild, or come not near me; noble, or not I for an angel; of good discourse, an excellent musician, and her hair shall be of what colour it please God. Ha! the prince and Monsieur Love! I will hide me in the arbour. [*Withdraws.*]

Enter Prince, Leonato, Claudio, and Balthazar, with Music.

D. Pedro. Come, shall we hear this music?
Claud. Yea, my good lord. How still the evening is,
As hush'd on purpose to grace harmony!
D. Pedro. See you where Benedick hath hid himself?
Claud. O! very well, my lord: the music ended,
We'll fit the kid-fox with a penny-worth.
D. Pedro. Come, Balthazar, we'll hear that song again.
Balth. O! good my lord, tax not so bad a voice
To slander music any more than once.

33 I'll none: *I'll have none of her* cheapen: *bargain for*
35 angel; *cf. n.* 37 of what colour, *etc.; cf. n.*
39 S. d. Balthazar; *cf. n.*
42 grace harmony: *do honor to music*
45 kid-fox; *cf. n.* penny-worth: *a good bargain*
47 tax: *impose a task*

D. Pedro. It is the witness still of excellency,
To put a strange face on his own perfection.
I pray thee, sing, and let me woo no more.

Balth. Because you talk of wooing, I will sing;
Since many a wooer doth commence his suit
To her he thinks not worthy; yet he woos;
Yet will he swear he loves.

D. Pedro. Nay, pray thee, come;
Or if thou wilt hold longer argument,
Do it in notes.

Balth. Note this before my notes;
There's not a note of mine that's worth the noting.

D. Pedro. Why these are very crotchets that he speaks;
Notes, notes, forsooth, and nothing! [*Music.*]

Bene. Now, divine air! now is his soul ravished! Is it not strange that sheeps' guts should hale souls out of men's bodies? Well, a horn for my money, when all's done.

The Song.

[*Balth.*]

'Sigh no more, ladies, sigh no more,
Men were deceivers ever;
One foot in sea, and one on shore,
To one thing constant never.
Then sigh not so,
But let them go,
And be you blithe and bonny,
Converting all your sounds of woe
Into Hey nonny, nonny.

49, 50 *Cf. n.* 51 woo: *entreat* 57 notes: *music*
59 crotchets; *cf. n.* 60 *Cf. n.*
62 sheeps' guts: *i.e. violin strings*

'Sing no more ditties, sing no mo
  Of dumps so dull and heavy;
The fraud of men was ever so,
  Since summer first was leavy.
    Then sigh not so,
    But let them go,
  And be you blithe and bonny,
Converting all your sounds of woe
  Into Hey nonny, nonny.'

D. Pedro. By my troth, a good song.

Balth. And an ill singer, my lord.

D. Pedro. Ha, no, no, faith; thou singest well enough for a shift.

Bene. [*Aside.*] An he had been a dog that should have howled thus, they would have hanged him; and I pray God his bad voice bode no mischief. I had as lief have heard the night-raven, come what plague could have come after it.

D. Pedro. Yea, marry. Dost thou hear, Balthazar? I pray thee, get us some excellent music, for to-morrow night we would have it at the Lady Hero's chamber-window.

Balth. The best I can, my lord.

D. Pedro. Do so: farewell. *Exit Balthazar.* Come hither, Leonato: what was it you told me of to-day, that your niece Beatrice was in love with Signior Benedick?

Claud. O! ay:—[*Aside to D. Pedro.*] Stalk on, stalk on; the fowl sits. I did never think that lady would have loved any man.

Leon. No, nor I neither; but most wonderful

74 mo: *more* 75 dumps: *mournful tunes* 77 leavy: *leafy*
86 shift: *makeshift* 90 night-raven; *cf. n.*
92 Yea, marry; *cf. n.* 101 Stalk on, *etc.*; *cf. n.*

that she should so dote on Signior Benedick, whom she hath in all outward behaviours seemed ever to abhor.

Bene. [*Aside.*] Is't possible? Sits the wind in that corner?

Leon. By my troth, my lord, I cannot tell what to think of it but that she loves him with an enraged affection: it is past the infinite of thought.

D. Pedro. May be she doth but counterfeit.

Claud. Faith, like enough.

Leon. O God! counterfeit! There was never counterfeit of passion came so near the life of passion as she discovers it.

D. Pedro. Why, what effects of passion shows she?

Claud. [*Aside.*] Bait the hook well: this fish will bite.

Leon. What effects, my lord? She will sit you—[*To Claudio.*] You heard my daughter tell you how.

Claud. She did, indeed.

D. Pedro. How, how, I pray you? You amaze me: I would have thought her spirit had been invincible against all assaults of affection.

Leon. I would have sworn it had, my lord; especially against Benedick.

Bene. [*Aside.*] I should think this a gull, but that the white-bearded fellow speaks it: knavery cannot, sure, hide itself in such reverence.

Claud. [*Aside.*] He hath ta'en the infection: hold it up.

112 enraged: *frenzied* infinite: *utmost power*
132 gull: *trick* 136 hold it up: *keep it up*

D. Pedro. Hath she made her affection known to Benedick?

Leon. No; and swears she never will: that's her torment. 140

Claud. 'Tis true, indeed; so your daughter says: 'Shall I,' says she, 'that have so oft encountered him with scorn, write to him that I love him?' 144

Leon. This says she now when she is beginning to write to him; for she'll be up twenty times a night, and there will she sit in her smock till she have writ a sheet of paper: my daughter tells us all. 149

Claud. Now you talk of a sheet of paper, I remember a pretty jest your daughter told us of.

Leon. O! when she had writ it, and was reading it over, she found Benedick and Beatrice between the sheet?

Claud. That. 155

Leon. O! she tore the letter into a thousand halfpence; railed at herself, that she should be so immodest to write to one that she knew would flout her: 'I measure him,' says she, 'by my own spirit; for I should flout him, if he writ to me; yea, though I love him, I should.' 161

Claud. Then down upon her knees she falls, weeps, sobs, beats her heart, tears her hair, prays, curses; 'O sweet Benedick! God give me patience!' 165

Leon. She doth indeed; my daughter says so; and the ecstasy hath so much overborne her, that my daughter is sometimes afeard she will

147 smock: *undergarment* 155 That: *That was it*
157 halfpence: *pieces small as silver halfpence*
167 ecstasy: *madness*

do a desperate outrage to herself. It is very true.

D. Pedro. It were good that Benedick knew of it by some other, if she will not discover it.

Claud. To what end? he would but make a sport of it and torment the poor lady worse.

D. Pedro. An he should, it were an alms to hang him. She's an excellent sweet lady, and, out of all suspicion, she is virtuous.

Claud. And she is exceeding wise.

D. Pedro. In everything but in loving Benedick.

Leon. O! my lord, wisdom and blood combating in so tender a body, we have ten proofs to one that blood hath the victory. I am sorry for her, as I have just cause, being her uncle and her guardian.

D. Pedro. I would she had bestowed this dotage on me; I would have daffed all other respects and made her half myself. I pray you, tell Benedick of it, and hear what a' will say.

Leon. Were it good, think you?

Claud. Hero thinks surely she will die; for she says she will die if he love her not, and she will die ere she make her love known, and she will die if he woo her, rather than she will bate one breath of her accustomed crossness.

D. Pedro. She doth well: if she should make tender of her love, 'tis very possible he'll scorn it; for the man,—as you know all,—hath a contemptible spirit.

169 outrage: *act of violence* 175 alms: *good deed*
177 out of: *beyond* 187 dotage: *doting* daffed: *put aside*
188 respects: *considerations* half myself: *my wife*
197 tender: *offer* 198 contemptible: *contemptuous*

Claud. He is a very proper man.

D. Pedro. He hath indeed a good outward happiness.

Claud. 'Fore God, and in my mind, very wise.

D. Pedro. He doth indeed show some sparks that are like wit.

Leon. And I take him to be valiant.

D. Pedro. As Hector, I assure you: and in the managing of quarrels you may say he is wise; for either he avoids them with great discretion, or undertakes them with a most Christian-like fear.

Leon. If he do fear God, a' must necessarily keep peace: if he break the peace, he ought to enter into a quarrel with fear and trembling.

D. Pedro. And so will he do; for the man doth fear God, howsoever it seems not in him by some large jests he will make. Well, I am sorry for your niece. Shall we go seek Benedick, and tell him of her love?

Claud. Never tell him, my lord: let her wear it out with good counsel.

Leon. Nay, that's impossible: she may wear her heart out first.

D. Pedro. Well, we will hear further of it by your daughter: let it cool the while. I love Benedick well, and I could wish he would modestly examine himself, to see how much he is unworthy to have so good a lady.

Leon. My lord, will you walk? dinner is ready.

Claud. [*Aside.*] If he do not dote on her upon this, I will never trust my expectation.

200 proper: *good-looking*
201 outward happiness: *lucky exterior*
217 large: *broad*
229 walk: *go*

D. Pedro. [*Aside.*] Let there be the same net spread for her; and that must your daughter and her gentlewoman carry. The sport will be, when they hold one an opinion of another's dotage, and no such matter: that's the scene that I would see, which will be merely a dumb-show. Let us send her to call him in to dinner.

Exeunt [*all but Benedick*].

Bene. [*Advancing from the arbour.*] This can be no trick: the conference was sadly borne. They have the truth of this from Hero. They seem to pity the lady: it seems, her affections have their full bent. Love me! why, it must be requited. I hear how I am censured: they say I will bear myself proudly, if I perceive the love come from her; they say too that she will rather die than give any sign of affection. I did never think to marry: I must not seem proud: happy are they that hear their detractions, and can put them to mending. They say the lady is fair: 'tis a truth, I can bear them witness; and virtuous: 'tis so, I cannot reprove it; and wise, but for loving me: by my troth, it is no addition to her wit, nor no great argument of her folly, for I will be horribly in love with her. I may chance have some odd quirks and remnants of wit broken on me, because I have railed so long against marriage; but doth not the appetite alter? A man loves the meat in his youth that he cannot en-

234 carry: *carry out*
236 no such matter: *nothing of the kind exists*
240 sadly borne: *seriously conducted*
243 full bent: *extreme tension*
249 put them to mending: *profit by them*
252 reprove: *disprove* 253 addition: *honor* 256 quirks: *jests*

dure in his age. Shall quips and sentences and these paper bullets of the brain awe a man from the career of his humour? No; the world must be peopled. When I said I would die a bachelor, I did not think I should live till I were married. Here comes Beatrice. By this day! she's a fair lady: I do spy some marks of love in her.

Enter Beatrice.

Beat. Against my will I am sent to bid you come in to dinner.

Bene. Fair Beatrice, I thank you for your pains.

Beat. I took no more pains for those thanks than you take pains to thank me: if it had been painful, I would not have come.

Bene. You take pleasure then in the message?

Beat. Yea, just so much as you may take upon a knife's point, and choke a daw withal. You have no stomach, signior: fare you well. *Exit.*

Bene. Ha! 'Against my will I am sent to bid you come in to dinner,' there's a double meaning in that. 'I took no more pains for those thanks than you took pains to thank me,' that's as much as to say, Any pains that I take for you is as easy as thanks. If I do not take pity of her, I am a villain; if I do not love her, I am a Jew. I will go get her picture. *Exit.*

260 quips: *sarcasms* sentences: *wise sayings*
261 paper bullets; *cf. n.*
276 choke . . withal: *more than a mouthful for a jackdaw*

ACT THIRD

Scene One

[*Leonato's Orchard*]

Enter Hero, Margaret, and Ursula.

Hero. Good Margaret, run thee to the parlour;
There shalt thou find my cousin Beatrice
Proposing with the prince and Claudio:
Whisper her ear, and tell her, I and Ursula
Walk in the orchard, and our whole discourse
Is all of her; say that thou overheard'st us,
And bid her steal into the pleached bower,
Where honey-suckles, ripen'd by the sun,
Forbid the sun to enter; like favourites,
Made proud by princes, that advance their pride
Against that power that bred it. There will she hide her,
To listen our propose. This is thy office;
Bear thee well in it and leave us alone.

Marg. I'll make her come, I warrant you, presently. [*Exit.*]

Hero. Now, Ursula, when Beatrice doth come,
As we do trace this alley up and down,
Our talk must only be of Benedick:
When I do name him, let it be thy part
To praise him more than ever man did merit.
My talk to thee must be how Benedick
Is sick in love with Beatrice: of this matter
Is little Cupid's crafty arrow made,
That only wounds by hearsay.

3 Proposing: *talking*
12 propose: *conversation*
16 trace: *traverse*
23 only . . hearsay: *hearsay alone*

Enter Beatrice [into the bower].

Now begin;
For look where Beatrice, like a lapwing, runs
Close by the ground, to hear our conference.
Urs. The pleasant'st angling is to see the fish
Cut with her golden oars the silver stream,
And greedily devour the treacherous bait:
So angle we for Beatrice; who even now
Is couched in the woodbine coverture.
Fear you not my part of the dialogue.
Hero. Then go we near her, that her ear lose nothing
Of the false sweet bait that we lay for it.

[*They advance towards the bower.*]

No, truly, Ursula, she is too disdainful;
I know her spirits are as coy and wild
As haggards of the rock.
Urs. But are you sure
That Benedick loves Beatrice so entirely?
Hero. So says the prince, and my new-trothed lord.
Urs. And did they bid you tell her of it, madam?
Hero. They did entreat me to acquaint her of it;
But I persuaded them, if they lov'd Benedick,
To wish him wrestle with affection,
And never to let Beatrice know of it.
Urs. Why did you so? Doth not the gentleman
Deserve as full as fortunate a bed
As ever Beatrice shall couch upon?

30 woodbine coverture: *honeysuckle bower*
36 haggards: *female hawks, grown up in freedom*
45 as full as; *cf. n.*

Hero. O god of love! I know he doth deserve
As much as may be yielded to a man;
But nature never fram'd a woman's heart
Of prouder stuff than that of Beatrice;
Disdain and scorn ride sparkling in her eyes,
Misprising what they look on, and her wit
Values itself so highly, that to her
All matter else seems weak. She cannot love
Nor take no shape nor project of affection,
She is so self-endear'd.

Urs. Sure, I think so;
And therefore certainly it were not good
She knew his love, lest she make sport at it.

Hero. Why, you speak truth. I never yet saw man,
How wise, how noble, young, how rarely featur'd,
But she would spell him backward: if fair-fac'd,
She would swear the gentleman should be her sister;
If black, why, Nature, drawing of an antic,
Made a foul blot; if tall, a lance ill-headed;
If low, an agate very vilely cut;
If speaking, why, a vane blown with all winds;
If silent, why, a block moved with none.
So turns she every man the wrong side out,
And never gives to truth and virtue that
Which simpleness and merit purchaseth.

Urs. Sure, sure, such carping is not commendable.

52 Misprising: *despising*
55 project: *idea*
56 self-endear'd: *full of self-love*
60 How: *however*
61 spell . . backward; *cf. n.*
63 black: *dark* antic: *grotesque figure*
65 agate: *human figure cut cameo-like on agate*
70 purchaseth: *deservedly obtain*

Hero. No; not to be so odd and from all fashions
As Beatrice is, cannot be commendable.
But who dare tell her so? If I should speak,
She would mock me into air: O! she would laugh me
Out of myself, press me to death with wit.
Therefore let Benedick, like cover'd fire,
Consume away in sighs, waste inwardly:
It were a better death than die with mocks,
Which is as bad as die with tickling.

Urs. Yet tell her of it: hear what she will say.

Hero. No; rather I will go to Benedick,
And counsel him to fight against his passion.
And, truly, I'll devise some honest slanders
To stain my cousin with. One doth not know
How much an ill word may empoison liking.

Urs. O! do not do your cousin such a wrong.
She cannot be so much without true judgment,—
Having so swift and excellent a wit
As she is priz'd to have,—as to refuse
So rare a gentleman as Signior Benedick.

Hero. He is the only man of Italy,
Always excepted my dear Claudio.

Urs. I pray you, be not angry with me, madam,
Speaking my fancy: Signior Benedick,
For shape, for bearing, argument and valour,
Goes foremost in report through Italy.

Hero. Indeed, he hath an excellent good name.

Urs. His excellence did earn it, ere he had it.
When are you married, madam?

72 from: *contrary to*
84 honest: *not injurious to character*
90 priz'd: *esteemed*
96 argument: *power of reason*

Hero. Why, every day—to-morrow. Come, go in:
I'll show thee some attires, and have thy counsel
Which is the best to furnish me to-morrow.
Urs. [*Aside to Hero.*] She's lim'd, I warrant you: we have caught her, madam. 104
Hero. [*Aside to Urs.*] If it prove so, then loving goes by haps:
Some Cupid kills with arrows, some with traps.
Exeunt Hero and Ursula.
Beat. [*Advancing.*] What fire is in mine ears? Can this be true? 107
Stand I condemn'd for pride and scorn so much?
Contempt, farewell! and maiden pride, adieu!
No glory lives behind the back of such.
And, Benedick, love on; I will requite thee,
Taming my wild heart to thy loving hand: 112
If thou dost love, my kindness shall incite thee
To bind our loves up in a holy band;
For others say thou dost deserve, and I
Believe it better than reportingly. *Exit.*

Scene Two

[*Leonato's House?*]

Enter Prince, Claudio, Benedick, and Leonato.

D. Pedro. I do but stay till your marriage be consummate, and then go I toward Arragon.

Claud. I'll bring you thither, my lord, if you'll vouchsafe me.

101 every day—to-morrow; *cf. n.* 104 lim'd: *snared*
105 haps: *chances* 110 behind the back; *cf. n.* 112 *Cf. n.*
114 band: *bond*
116 better . . reportingly: *on better evidence than report*

D. Pedro. Nay, that would be as great a soil in the new gloss of your marriage, as to show a child his new coat and forbid him to wear it. I will only be bold with Benedick for his company; for, from the crown of his head to the sole of his foot, he is all mirth: he hath twice or thrice cut Cupid's bow-string, and the little hangman dare not shoot at him. He hath a heart as sound as a bell, and his tongue is the clapper; for what his heart thinks his tongue speaks.

Bene. Gallants, I am not as I have been.

Leon. So say I: methinks you are sadder.

Claud. I hope he be in love.

D. Pedro. Hang him, truant! there's no true drop of blood in him, to be truly touched with love. If he be sad, he wants money.

Bene. I have the tooth-ache.

D. Pedro. Draw it.

Bene. Hang it.

Claud. You must hang it first, and draw it afterwards.

D. Pedro. What! sigh for the tooth-ache?

Leon. Where is but a humour or a worm?

Bene. Well, every one can master a grief but he that has it.

Claud. Yet say I, he is in love.

D. Pedro. There is no appearance of fancy in him, unless it be a fancy that he hath to strange disguises; as, to be a Dutchman to-day, a Frenchman to-morrow, or in the shape of two countries at once, as a German from the waist downward, all slops, and a Spaniard from the hip upward,

11 hangman: *rogue* 24 hang . . draw; *cf. n.*
27 worm; *cf. n.* 31 fancy: *love* 36 slops: *loose breeches*

no doublet. Unless he have a fancy to this foolery, as it appears he hath, he is no fool for fancy, as you would have it appear he is. 39

Claud. If he be not in love with some woman, there is no believing old signs: a' brushes his hat a mornings; what should that bode?

D. Pedro. Hath any man seen him at the barber's? 44

Claud. No, but the barber's man hath been seen with him; and the old ornament of his cheek hath already stuffed tennis-balls.

Leon. Indeed he looks younger than he did, by the loss of a beard. 49

D. Pedro. Nay, a' rubs himself with civet: can you smell him out by that?

Claud. That's as much as to say the sweet youth's in love. 53

D. Pedro. The greatest note of it is his melancholy.

Claud. And when was he wont to wash his face? 57

D. Pedro. Yea, or to paint himself? for the which, I hear what they say of him.

Claud. Nay, but his jesting spirit; which is now crept into a lute-string, and new-governed by stops.

D. Pedro. Indeed, that tells a heavy tale for him. Conclude, conclude he is in love. 64

Claud. Nay, but I know who loves him.

D. Pedro. That would I know too: I warrant, one that knows him not.

37 no doublet; *cf. n.* 46 the old ornament, *etc.; cf. n.*
50 civet: *a perfume*
62 stops: *frets, regulating the sound of the lutestring*

Claud. Yes, and his ill conditions; and in despite of all, dies for him.

D. Pedro. She shall be buried with her face upwards.

Bene. Yet is this no charm for the tooth-ache. Old signior, walk aside with me: I have studied eight or nine wise words to speak to you, which these hobby-horses must not hear.

[*Exeunt Benedick and Leonato.*]

D. Pedro. For my life, to break with him about Beatrice.

Claud. 'Tis even so. Hero and Margaret have by this played their parts with Beatrice, and then the two bears will not bite one another when they meet.

Enter John the Bastard.

D. John. My lord and brother, God save you!

D. Pedro. Good den, brother.

D. John. If your leisure served, I would speak with you.

D. Pedro. In private?

D. John. If it please you; yet Count Claudio may hear, for what I would speak of concerns him.

D. Pedro. What's the matter?

D. John. [*To Claudio.*] Means your lordship to be married to-morrow?

D. Pedro. You know he does.

D. John. I know not that, when he knows what I know.

68 conditions: *characteristics*
70 buried, *etc.; cf. n.*
75 hobby-horses; *cf. n.*
83 Good den: *Good even(ing)*
90 *Cf. n.*

Claud. If there be any impediment, I pray you discover it.

D. John. You may think I love you not: let that appear hereafter, and aim better at me by that I now will manifest. For my brother, I think he holds you well, and in dearness of heart hath holp to effect your ensuing marriage; surely suit ill spent, and labour ill bestowed!

D. Pedro. Why, what's the matter?

D. John. I came hither to tell you; and circumstances shortened,—for she hath been too long a talking of,—the lady is disloyal.

Claud. Who, Hero?

D. John. Even she: Leonato's Hero, your Hero, every man's Hero.

Claud. Disloyal?

D. John. The word's too good to paint out her wickedness; I could say, she were worse: think you of a worse title, and I will fit her to it. Wonder not till further warrant: go but with me to-night, you shall see her chamber-window entered, even the night before her wedding-day: if you love her then, to-morrow wed her; but it would better fit your honour to change your mind.

Claud. May this be so?

D. Pedro. I will not think it.

D. John. If you dare not trust that you see, confess not that you know. If you will follow me, I will show you enough; and when you have seen more and heard more, proceed accordingly.

99 aim . . at: *judge of*
101 holds: *esteems* dearness: *affection*
106 circumstances shortened: *cutting short the particulars*
107 a talking of: *under discussion* 112 paint out: *depict*
115 till . . warrant: *till further proof appears* 123 that: *what*

Claud. If I see any thing to-night why I should not marry her to-morrow, in the congregation, where I should wed, there will I shame her.

D. Pedro. And, as I wooed for thee to obtain her, I will join with thee to disgrace her.

D. John. I will disparage her no further till you are my witnesses: bear it coldly but till midnight, and let the issue show itself.

D. Pedro. O day untowardly turned!

Claud. O mischief strangely thwarting!

D. John. O plague right well prevented! So will you say when you have seen the sequel.

Exeunt.

Scene Three

[*A Street*]

Enter Dogberry and his compartner [*Verges*], *with the watch.*

Dogb. Are you good men and true?

Verg. Yea, or else it were pity but they should suffer salvation, body and soul.

Dogb. Nay, that were a punishment too good for them, if they should have any allegiance in them, being chosen for the prince's watch.

Verg. Well, give them their charge, neighbour Dogberry.

Dogb. First, who think you the most desartless man to be constable?

First Watch. Hugh Oatcake, sir, or George Seacoal; for they can write and read.

136 untowardly turned: *unluckily altered*
Sc. iii., S. d. watch: *night watchmen*
3 salvation: *i.e. damnation* 9 desartless: *i.e. deserving*

Dogb. Come hither, neighbour Seacoal. God hath blessed you with a good name: to be a well-favoured man is the gift of fortune; but to write and read comes by nature.

Sec. Watch. Both which, Master constable,—

Dogb. You have: I knew it would be your answer. Well, for your favour, sir, why, give God thanks, and make no boast of it; and for your writing and reading, let that appear when there is no need of such vanity. You are thought here to be the most senseless and fit man for the constable of the watch; therefore bear you the lantern. This is your charge: you shall comprehend all vagrom men; you are to bid any man stand, in the prince's name.

Watch. How, if a' will not stand?

Dogb. Why, then, take no note of him, but let him go; and presently call the rest of the watch together, and thank God you are rid of a knave.

Verg. If he will not stand when he is bidden, he is none of the prince's subjects.

Dogb. True, and they are to meddle with none but the prince's subjects. You shall also make no noise in the streets: for, for the watch to babble and to talk is most tolerable and not to be endured.

Sec. Watch. We will rather sleep than talk: we know what belongs to a watch.

Dogb. Why, you speak like an ancient and most quiet watchman, for I cannot see how sleeping should offend; only have a care that your bills be not stolen. Well, you are to call

15 well-favoured: *good-looking*
25 comprehend: *i.e. apprehend*
26 vagrom: *vagrant* 40 belongs to: *befits* 44 bills: *pikes*

at all the alehouses, and bid those that are drunk get them to bed.

Watch. How if they will not?

Dogb. Why then, let them alone till they are sober: if they make you not then the better answer, you may say they are not the men you took them for.

Watch. Well, sir.

Dogb. If you meet a thief, you may suspect him, by virtue of your office, to be no true man; and, for such kind of men, the less you meddle or make with them, why, the more is for your honesty.

Sec. Watch. If we know him to be a thief, shall we not lay hands on him?

Dogb. Truly, by your office, you may; but I think they that touch pitch will be defiled. The most peaceable way for you, if you do take a thief, is, to let him show himself what he is and steal out of your company.

Verg. You have been always called a merciful man, partner.

Dogb. Truly, I would not hang a dog by my will, much more a man who hath any honesty in him.

Verg. If you hear a child cry in the night, you must call to the nurse and bid her still it.

Sec. Watch. How if the nurse be asleep and will not hear us?

Dogb. Why, then, depart in peace, and let the child wake her with crying; for the ewe that will not hear her lamb when it baes, will never answer a calf when he bleats.

Verg. 'Tis very true.

54 true: *honest* 56 meddle or make: *have to do* is: (*it*) *is*

Dogb. This is the end of the charge. You, constable, are to present the prince's own person: if you meet the prince in the night, you may stay him.

Verg. Nay, by 'r lady, that I think, a' cannot.

Dogb. Five shillings to one on 't, with any man that knows the statues, he may stay him: marry, not without the prince be willing; for, indeed, the watch ought to offend no man, and it is an offence to stay a man against his will.

Verg. By 'r lady, I think it be so.

Dogb. Ha, ah, ha! Well, masters, good night: an there be any matter of weight chances, call up me: keep your fellows' counsels and your own, and good night. Come, neighbour.

Sec. Watch. Well, masters, we hear our charge: let us go sit here upon the church-bench till two, and then all go to bed.

Dogb. One word more, honest neighbours. I pray you, watch about Signior Leonato's door; for the wedding being there to-morrow, there is a great coil to-night. Adieu; be vigitant, I beseech you. *Exeunt* [*Dogberry and Verges*].

Enter Borachio and Conrade.

Bora. What, Conrade!

Watch. [*Aside.*] Peace! stir not.

Bora. Conrade, I say!

Con. Here, man, I am at thy elbow.

Bora. Mass, and my elbow itched; I thought there would a scab follow.

79 present: *represent* 84 statues: *i.e. statutes*
94 church-bench: *bench outside the church*
99 coil: *bustle* vigitant: *i.e. vigilant*
105 Mass: *by the Mass!* 106 scab; *cf. n.*

Con. I will owe thee an answer for that; and now forward with thy tale.

Bora. Stand thee close then under this pent-house, for it drizzles rain, and I will, like a true drunkard, utter all to thee.

Watch. [*Aside.*] Some treason, masters; yet stand close.

Bora. Therefore know, I have earned of Don John a thousand ducats.

Con. Is it possible that any villainy should be so dear?

Bora. Thou shouldst rather ask if it were possible any villainy should be so rich; for when rich villains have need of poor ones, poor ones may make what price they will.

Con. I wonder at it.

Bora. That shows thou art unconfirmed. Thou knowest that the fashion of a doublet, or a hat, or a cloak, is nothing to a man.

Con. Yes, it is apparel.

Bora. I mean, the fashion.

Con. Yes, the fashion is the fashion.

Bora. Tush! I may as well say the fool's the fool. But seest thou not what a deformed thief this fashion is?

Watch. [*Aside.*] I know that Deformed; a' has been a vile thief this seven years; a' goes up and down like a gentleman: I remember his name.

Bora. Didst thou not hear somebody?

Con. No: 'twas the vane on the house.

Bora. Seest thou not, I say, what a deformed

109 pent-house: *projecting roof*
113 stand close: *keep concealed*
123 unconfirmed: *inexperienced*

thief this fashion is? how giddily he turns about all the hot bloods between fourteen and five-and-thirty? sometime fashioning them like Pharaoh's soldiers in the reechy painting; sometime like god Bel's priests in the old church-window; sometime like the shaven Hercules in the smirched worm-eaten tapestry, where his cod-piece seems as massy as his club?

Con. All this I see, and I see that the fashion wears out more apparel than the man. But art not thou thyself giddy with the fashion too, that thou hast shifted out of thy tale into telling me of the fashion?

Bora. Not so, neither; but know, that I have to-night wooed Margaret, the Lady Hero's gentle-woman, by the name of Hero: she leans me out at her mistress' chamber-window, bids me a thousand times good night,—I tell this tale vilely:—I should first tell thee how the prince, Claudio, and my master, planted and placed and possessed by my master Don John, saw afar off in the orchard this amiable encounter.

Con. And thought they Margaret was Hero?

Bora. Two of them did, the prince and Claudio; but the devil my master, knew she was Margaret; and partly by his oaths, which first possessed them, partly by the dark night, which did deceive them, but chiefly by my villainy, which did confirm any slander that Don John had made, away went Claudio enraged; swore he would meet her, as he was appointed, next morning at the temple, and there, before the

142 reechy: *dirty, stained with smoke* 143 Bel's priests; *cf. n.*
145 cod-piece: *part of Elizabethan breeches*
147 the fashion, *etc.; cf. n.* 159 possessed: *influenced*

whole congregation, shame her with what he saw o'er night, and send her home again without a husband. 173

First Watch. We charge you in the prince's name, stand!

Sec. Watch. Call up the right Master constable. We have here recovered the most dangerous piece of lechery that ever was known in the commonwealth.

First Watch. And one Deformed is one of
them: I know him, a' wears a lock. 181

Con. Masters, masters!

Sec. Watch. You'll be made bring Deformed
forth, I warrant you. 184

Con. Masters,—

First Watch. Never speak: we charge you let us obey you to go with us.

Bora. We are like to prove a goodly commodity, being taken up of these men's bills. 189

Con. A commodity in question, I warrant you. Come, we'll obey you. *Exeunt.*

Scene Four

[*Hero's Apartment*]

Enter Hero, Margaret, and Ursula.

Hero. Good Ursula, wake my cousin Beatrice, and desire her to rise.

Urs. I will, lady.

Hero. And bid her come hither. 4

Urs. Well. [*Exit.*]

176 right Master; *cf. n.*
177 recovered: *i.e. discovered*
181 lock: *love-lock (of hair)*
188 commodity; *cf. n.*
190 in question: *subject to trial*

Marg. Troth, I think your other rabato were better.

Hero. No, pray thee, good Meg, I'll wear this.

Marg. By my troth's not so good; and I warrant your cousin will say so.

Hero. My cousin's a fool, and thou art another: I'll wear none but this.

Marg. I like the new tire within excellently, if the hair were a thought browner; and your gown's a most rare fashion, i' faith. I saw the Duchess of Milan's gown that they praise so.

Hero. O! that exceeds, they say.

Marg. By my troth's but a night-gown in respect of yours: cloth o' gold, and cuts, and laced with silver, set with pearls, down sleeves, side sleeves, and skirts round, underborne with a bluish tinsel; but for a fine, quaint, graceful, and excellent fashion, yours is worth ten on 't.

Hero. God give me joy to wear it! for my heart is exceeding heavy.

Marg. 'Twill be heavier soon by the weight of a man.

Hero. Fie upon thee! art not ashamed?

Marg. Of what, lady? of speaking honourably? is not marriage honourable in a beggar? Is not your lord honourable without marriage? I think you would have me say, 'saving your reverence, a husband:' an bad thinking do not wrest true speaking, I'll offend nobody. Is there

6 rabato: *stiff collar* 9 troth's: *i.e. troth, it is*
13 tire: *headdress* within; *cf. n.*
18 night-gown: *'tea-gown'* in respect of: *compared with*
19 cuts: *slashed openings, showing the fabric underneath*
20 laced: *trimmed* down sleeves: *tight-fitting sleeves* (?)
21 side sleeves: *long outer sleeves, open from the shoulder* underborne: *lined*
32 saving your reverence; *cf. n.* 34 wrest: *distort*

any harm in 'the heavier for a husband?' None, I think, an it be the right husband and the right wife; otherwise 'tis light, and not heavy: ask my Lady Beatrice else; here she comes.

Enter Beatrice.

Hero. Good morrow, coz.

Beat. Good morrow, sweet Hero.

Hero. Why, how now! do you speak in the sick tune?

Beat. I am out of all other tune, methinks.

Marg. Clap's into 'Light o' love;' that goes without a burden: do you sing it, and I'll dance it.

Beat. Ye light o' love with your heels! then, if your husband have stables enough, you'll see he shall lack no barns.

Marg. O illegitimate construction! I scorn that with my heels.

Beat. 'Tis almost five o'clock, cousin; 'tis time you were ready. By my troth, I am exceeding ill. Heigh-ho!

Marg. For a hawk, a horse, or a husband?

Beat. For the letter that begins them all, H.

Marg. Well, an you be not turned Turk, there's no more sailing by the star.

Beat. What means the fool, trow?

Marg. Nothing I; but God send every one their heart's desire!

Hero. These gloves the count sent me; they are an excellent perfume.

37 light: *wanton (pun)* 42 sick tune: *tone of an invalid*
44 'Light o' love': *a popular song*
45 burden: *bass accompaniment*
48 barns: *pun on bairns, children*
50 with my heels: *as if by kicking*
55 H: *pronounced much like 'ache'*
56 turned Turk: *become renegade* 58 trow: *(do you) think?*

Beat. I am stuffed, cousin, I cannot smell.

Marg. A maid, and stuffed! there's goodly catching of cold.

Beat. O, God help me! God help me! how long have you professed apprehension?

Marg. Ever since you left it. Doth not my wit become me rarely!

Beat. It is not seen enough, you should wear it in your cap. By my troth, I am sick.

Marg. Get you some of this distilled Carduus Benedictus, and lay it to your heart: it is the only thing for a qualm.

Hero. There thou prick'st her with a thistle.

Beat. Benedictus! why Benedictus? you have some moral in this Benedictus.

Marg. Moral! no, by my troth, I have no moral meaning; I meant, plain holy-thistle. You may think, perchance, that I think you are in love: nay, by'r lady, I am not such a fool to think what I list; nor I list not to think what I can; nor, indeed, I cannot think, if I would think my heart out of thinking, that you are in love, or that you will be in love, or that you can be in love. Yet Benedick was such another, and now is he become a man: he swore he would never marry; and yet now, in despite of his heart, he eats his meat without grudging: and how you may be converted, I know not; but methinks you look with your eyes as other women do.

Beat. What pace is this that thy tongue keeps?

Marg. Not a false gallop.

67 professed apprehension: *made wit your profession*
72 Carduus Benedictus: *holy thistle, used in medicine*
77 moral: *hidden meaning* 82 list: *like* 94 false gallop: *canter*

Enter Ursula.

Urs. Madam, withdraw: the prince, the count, Signior Benedick, Don John, and all the gallants of the town, are come to fetch you to church.

Hero. Help to dress me, good coz, good Meg, good Ursula. [*Exeunt.*]

Scene Five

[*Another Room in Leonato's House*]

Enter Leonato and the Constable [*Dogberry*], *and the Headborough* [*Verges*].

Leon. What would you with me, honest neighbour?

Dogb. Marry, sir, I would have some confidence with you, that decerns you nearly.

Leon. Brief, I pray you; for you see it is a busy time with me.

Dogb. Marry, this it is, sir.

Verg. Yes, in truth it is, sir.

Leon. What is it, my good friends?

Dogb. Goodman Verges, sir, speaks a little off the matter: an old man, sir, and his wits are not so blunt, as, God help, I would desire they were; but, in faith, honest as the skin between his brows.

Verg. Yes, I thank God, I am as honest as any man living, that is an old man and no honester than I.

Dogb. Comparisons are odorous: palabras, neighbour Verges.

Sc. v., S. d. Headborough: *petty constable*
3 confidence: *i.e. conference* 4 decerns: *i.e. concerns*
10 Goodman: *yeoman; a rustic title*
18 odorous: *i.e. odious* palabras; *cf. n.*

Leon. Neighbours, you are tedious.

Dogb. It pleases your worship to say so, but we are the poor duke's officers; but truly, for mine own part, if I were as tedious as a king, I could find in my heart to bestow it all of your worship.

Leon. All thy tediousness on me! ha?

Dogb. Yea, an 't were a thousand pound more than 'tis; for I hear as good exclamation on your worship, as of any man in the city, and though I be but a poor man, I am glad to hear it.

Verg. And so am I.

Leon. I would fain know what you have to say.

Verg. Marry, sir, our watch to-night, excepting your worship's presence, ha' ta'en a couple of as arrant knaves as any in Messina.

Dogb. A good old man, sir; he will be talking: as they say, 'when the age is in, the wit is out.' God help us! it is a world to see! Well said, i' faith, neighbour Verges: well, God's a good man; an two men ride of a horse, one must ride behind. An honest soul, i' faith, sir; by my troth he is, as ever broke bread: but God is to be worshipped: all men are not alike; alas! good neighbour.

Leon. Indeed, neighbour, he comes too short of you.

Dogb. Gifts that God gives.

Leon. I must leave you.

Dogb. One word, sir: our watch, sir, hath indeed comprehended two aspicious persons, and

22 poor duke's: *i.e. duke's poor*
24 of: *on*
28 exclamation: *i.e. acclamation* (?)
33 to-night: *last night*
37 when the age is in, *etc.; cf. n.*
38 a world: *a wonder*
39 God's a good man; *cf. n.*
50 aspicious: *i.e. suspicious*

we would have them this morning examined before your worship.

Leon. Take their examination yourself, and bring it me: I am now in great haste, as may appear unto you.

Dogb. It shall be suffigance.

Leon. Drink some wine ere you go: fare you well.

[*Enter a Messenger.*]

Mess. My lord, they stay for you to give your daughter to her husband.

Leon. I'll wait upon them: I am ready.

[*Exeunt Leonato and Messenger.*]

Dogb. Go, good partner, go, get you to Francis Seacoal; bid him bring his pen and inkhorn to the gaol: we are now to examination these men.

Verg. And we must do it wisely.

Dogb. We will spare for no wit, I warrant you; here's that shall drive some of them to a *non-come:* only get the learned writer to set down our excommunication, and meet me at the gaol. *Exeunt.*

ACT FOURTH

Scene One

[*Within a Church*]

Enter Prince, Bastard, Leonato, Friar [Francis], Claudio, Benedick, Hero, and Beatrice.

Leon. Come, Friar Francis, be brief: only to

56 suffigance: *i.e. sufficient* 61 wait upon: *attend*
68 non-come; *cf. n.*
69 excommunication: *i.e. examination* or *communication*

the plain form of marriage, and you shall recount their particular duties afterwards.

Friar. You come hither, my lord, to marry this lady?

Claud. No.

Leon. To be married to her, friar; you come to marry her.

Friar. Lady, you come hither to be married to this count?

Hero. I do.

Friar. If either of you know any inward impediment, why you should not be conjoined, I charge you, on your souls, to utter it.

Claud. Know you any, Hero?

Hero. None, my lord.

Friar. Know you any, count?

Leon. I dare make his answer; none.

Claud. O! what men dare do! what men may do! what men daily do, not knowing what they do!

Bene. How now! Interjections? Why then, some be of laughing, as ah! ha! he!

Claud. Stand thee by, friar. Father, by your leave:
Will you with free and unconstrained soul
Give me this maid, your daughter?

Leon. As freely, son, as God did give her me.

Claud. And what have I to give you back whose worth
May counterpoise this rich and precious gift?

D. Pedro. Nothing, unless you render her again.

22 some . . laughing, *etc.; cf. n.* 28 counterpoise: *balance*
29 render: *give back*

Claud. Sweet prince, you learn me noble thankfulness.
There, Leonato, take her back again:
Give not this rotten orange to your friend;
She's but the sign and semblance of her honour.
Behold! how like a maid she blushes here.
O! what authority and show of truth
Can cunning sin cover itself withal.
Comes not that blood as modest evidence
To witness simple virtue? Would you not swear,
All you that see her, that she were a maid,
By these exterior shows? But she is none:
She knows the heat of a luxurious bed;
Her blush is guiltiness, not modesty.
Leon. What do you mean, my lord?
Claud. Not to be married,
Not to knit my soul to an approved wanton.
Leon. Dear my lord, if you, in your own proof,
Have vanquish'd the resistance of her youth,
And made defeat of her virginity,—
Claud. I know what you would say: if I have known her,
You'll say she did embrace me as a husband,
And so extenuate the 'forehand sin:
No, Leonato,
I never tempted her with word too large;
But, as a brother to his sister, show'd
Bashful sincerity and comely love.
Hero. And seem'd I ever otherwise to you?
Claud. Out on thee! Seeming! I will write against it:
You seem to me as Dian in her orb,

35 authority: *authenticity* 41 luxurious: *lustful*
45 in your own proof; *cf. n.* 50 'forehand sin: *sin of over-haste*
57 Dian in her orb: *the chaste Diana, enthroned in the moon*

As chaste as is the bud ere it be blown;
But you are more intemperate in your blood
Than Venus, or those pamper'd animals
That rage in savage sensuality.

Hero. Is my lord well, that he doth speak so wide?

Leon. Sweet prince, why speak not you?

D. Pedro. What should I speak?
I stand dishonour'd, that have gone about
To link my dear friend to a common stale.

Leon. Are these things spoken, or do I but dream?

D. John. Sir, they are spoken, and these things are true.

Bene. This looks not like a nuptial.

Hero. True! O God!

Claud. Leonato, stand I here?
Is this the prince? Is this the prince's brother?
Is this face Hero's? Are our eyes our own?

Leon. All this is so; but what of this, my lord?

Claud. Let me but move one question to your daughter;
And by that fatherly and kindly power
That you have in her, bid her answer truly.

Leon. I charge thee do so, as thou art my child.

Hero. O, God defend me! how am I beset!
What kind of catechizing call you this?

Claud. To make you answer truly to your name.

Hero. Is it not Hero? Who can blot that name

62 wide: *wide of the mark, incorrectly* 69 True! *cf. n.*
75 kindly: *natural*

With any just reproach?
Claud. Marry, that can Hero:
Hero itself can blot out Hero's virtue.
What man was he talk'd with you yesternight
Out at your window, betwixt twelve and one?
Now, if you are a maid, answer to this.
Hero. I talk'd with no man at that hour, my lord.
D. Pedro. Why, then are you no maiden. Leonato,
I am sorry you must hear: upon mine honour,
Myself, my brother, and this grieved count,
Did see her, hear her, at that hour last night,
Talk with a ruffian at her chamber-window;
Who hath indeed, most like a liberal villain
Confess'd the vile encounters they have had
A thousand times in secret.
D. John. Fie, fie! they are not to be nam'd, my lord,
Not to be spoke of;
There is not chastity enough in language
Without offence to utter them. Thus, pretty lady,
I am sorry for thy much misgovernment.
Claud. O Hero! what a Hero hadst thou been,
If half thy outward graces had been plac'd
About thy thoughts and counsels of thy heart!
But fare thee well, most foul, most fair! farewell,
Thou pure impiety, and impious purity!
For thee I'll lock up all the gates of love,
And on my eyelids shall conjecture hang,

83 Hero itself, *etc.; cf. n.*
93 liberal: *gross*
100 much misgovernment: *great misconduct*
107 conjecture: *suspicion*

To turn all beauty into thoughts of harm,
And never shall it more be gracious.

Leon. Hath no man's dagger here a point for me? [*Hero swoons.*]

Beat. Why, how now, cousin! wherefore sink you down?

D. John. Come, let us go. These things, come thus to light,
Smother her spirits up.

[*Exeunt Don Pedro, Don John and Claudio.*]

Bene. How doth the lady?

Beat. Dead, I think! help, uncle!
Hero! why, Hero! Uncle! Signior Benedick!
Friar!

Leon. O Fate! take not away thy heavy hand:
Death is the fairest cover for her shame
That may be wish'd for.

Beat. How now, cousin Hero!

Friar. Have comfort, lady.

Leon. Dost thou look up?

Friar. Yea; wherefore should she not?

Leon. Wherefore! Why, doth not every earthly thing
Cry shame upon her? Could she here deny
The story that is printed in her blood?
Do not live, Hero; do not ope thine eyes;
For, did I think thou wouldst not quickly die,
Thought I thy spirits were stronger than thy shames,
Myself would, on the rearward of reproaches,
Strike at thy life. Griev'd I, I had but one?
Chid I for that at frugal nature's frame?

109 gracious: *attractive*
128 on the rearward of: *following after*
130 frame: *established order*

O! one too much by thee. Why had I one?
Why ever wast thou lovely in mine eyes?
Why had I not with charitable hand
Took up a beggar's issue at my gates,
Who smirched thus, and mir'd with infamy,
I might have said, 'No part of it is mine;
This shame derives itself from unknown loins?'
But mine, and mine I lov'd, and mine I prais'd,
And mine that I was proud on, mine so much
That I myself was to myself not mine,
Valuing of her; why, she—O! she is fallen
Into a pit of ink, that the wide sea
Hath drops too few to wash her clean again,
And salt too little which may season give
To her foul-tainted flesh.

Bene. Sir, sir, be patient.
For my part, I am so attir'd in wonder,
I know not what to say.

Beat. O! on my soul, my cousin is belied!

Bene. Lady, were you her bedfellow last night?

Beat. No, truly, not; although, until last night,
I have this twelvemonth been her bedfellow.

Leon. Confirm'd, confirm'd! O! that is stronger made,
Which was before barr'd up with ribs of iron.
Would the two princes lie? and Claudio lie,
Who lov'd her so, that, speaking of her foulness,
Wash'd it with tears? Hence from her! let her die.

Friar. Hear me a little;
For I have only been silent so long,

140 *Cf. n.* 141 Valuing: *when estimating the value*
142 that: *so that* 144 season: *savor* 146 attir'd: *wrapped up*

And given way unto this course of fortune,
By noting of the lady: I have mark'd
A thousand blushing apparitions
To start into her face; a thousand innocent shames
In angel whiteness bear away those blushes;
And in her eye there hath appear'd a fire,
To burn the errors that these princes hold
Against her maiden truth. Call me a fool;
Trust not my reading nor my observations,
Which with experimental seal doth warrant
The tenour of my book; trust not my age,
My reverence, calling, nor divinity,
If this sweet lady lie not guiltless here
Under some biting error.

Leon. Friar, it cannot be.
Thou seest that all the grace that she hath left
Is, that she will not add to her damnation
A sin of perjury: she not denies it.
Why seek'st thou then to cover with excuse
That which appears in proper nakedness?

Friar. Lady. what man is he you are accus'd of?

Hero. They know that do accuse me, I know none;
If I know more of any man alive
Than that which maiden modesty doth warrant,
Let all my sins lack mercy! O, my father!
Prove you that any man with me convers'd
At hours unmeet, or that I yesternight
Maintain'd the change of words with any creature,

168 experimental seal: *seal of experience* 169 book; *cf. n.*
185 change: *exchange*

Refuse me, hate me, torture me to death.
Friar. There is some strange misprision in the princes.
Bene. Two of them have the very bent of honour;
And if their wisdoms be misled in this,
The practice of it lives in John the bastard,
Whose spirits toil in frame of villainies.
Leon. I know not. If they speak but truth of her,
These hands shall tear her; if they wrong her honour,
The proudest of them shall well hear of it.
Time hath not yet so dried this blood of mine,
Nor age so eat up my invention,
Nor fortune made such havoc of my means,
Nor my bad life reft me so much of friends,
But they shall find, awak'd in such a kind,
Both strength of limb and policy of mind,
Ability in means and choice of friends,
To quit me of them throughly.
Friar. Pause awhile,
And let my counsel sway you in this case.
Your daughter here the princes left for dead;
Let her awhile be secretly kept in,
And publish it that she is dead indeed:
Maintain a mourning ostentation;
And on your family's old monument
Hang mournful epitaphs and do all rites
That appertain unto a burial.

187 misprision: *misunderstanding*
188 bent: *natural inclination*
190 practice: *trickery*
191 frame: *contrivance*
196 invention: *power of mind*
199 kind: *manner*
202 quit . . of: *avenge . . on*
205 secretly kept in: *kept hidden*
207 mourning ostentation: *show of mourning*

Leon. What shall become of this? What will this do?
Friar. Marry, this well carried shall on her behalf
Change slander to remorse; that is some good:
But not for that dream I on this strange course,
But on this travail look for greater birth.
She dying, as it must be so maintain'd,
Upon the instant that she was accus'd,
Shall be lamented, pitied and excus'd
Of every hearer; for it so falls out
That what we have we prize not to the worth
Whiles we enjoy it, but being lack'd and lost,
Why, then we rack the value, then we find
The virtue that possession would not show us
Whiles it was ours. So will it fare with Claudio:
When he shall hear she died upon his words,
The idea of her life shall sweetly creep
Into his study of imagination,
And every lovely organ of her life
Shall come apparell'd in more precious habit,
More moving-delicate, and full of life
Into the eye and prospect of his soul,
Than when she liv'd indeed: then shall he mourn,—
If ever love had interest in his liver,—
And wish he had not so accused her,
No, though he thought his accusation true.
Let this be so, and doubt not but success
Will fashion the event in better shape
Than I can lay it down in likelihood.

222 rack: *stretch* 227 study of imagination: *imaginative study*
228 organ: *faculty* 229 habit: *dress*
230 moving-delicate: *touchingly delicate* 231 prospect: *view*
233 liver: *supposed seat of love* 236 success: *the result*
238 lay . . likelihood: *conjecture*

But if all aim but this be levell'd false,
The supposition of the lady's death
Will quench the wonder of her infamy:
And if it sort not well, you may conceal her,—
As best befits her wounded reputation,—
In some reclusive and religious life,
Out of all eyes, tongues, minds and injuries.

Bene. Signior Leonato, let the friar advise you:
And though you know my inwardness and love
Is very much unto the prince and Claudio,
Yet, by mine honour, I will deal in this
As secretly and justly as your soul
Should with your body.

Leon. Being that I flow in grief,
The smallest twine may lead me.

Friar. 'Tis well consented: presently away;
For to strange sores strangely they strain the cure.
Come, lady, die to live: this wedding day
Perhaps is but prolong'd: have patience and endure.

Exit [*with Leonato and Hero.*]

Bene. Lady Beatrice, have you wept all this while?

Beat. Yea, and I will weep a while longer.

Bene. I will not desire that.

Beat. You have no reason; I do it freely.

Bene. Surely I do believe your fair cousin is wronged.

Beat. Ah! how much might the man deserve of me that would right her.

239 *Cf. n.* 242 sort: *turn out* 244 reclusive: *secluded*
245 injuries: *insults* 247 inwardness: *intimacy*
251 flow in: *overflow with* 254 *Cf. n.*
256 prolong'd: *postponed*

Bene. Is there any way to show such friendship?

Beat. A very even way, but no such friend.

Bene. May a man do it?

Beat. It is a man's office, but not yours.

Bene. I do love nothing in the world so well as you: is not that strange?

Beat. As strange as the thing I know not. It were as possible for me to say I loved nothing so well as you; but believe me not, and yet I lie not; I confess nothing, nor I deny nothing. I am sorry for my cousin.

Bene. By my sword, Beatrice, thou lovest me.

Beat. Do not swear by it, and eat it.

Bene. I will swear by it that you love me; and I will make him eat it that says I love not you.

Beat. Will you not eat your word?

Bene. With no sauce that can be devised to it. I protest I love thee.

Beat. Why then, God forgive me!

Bene. What offence, sweet Beatrice?

Beat. You have stayed me in a happy hour: I was about to protest I loved you.

Bene. And do it with all thy heart.

Beat. I love you with so much of my heart that none is left to protest.

Bene. Come, bid me do anything for thee.

Beat. Kill Claudio.

Bene. Ha! not for the wide world.

Beat. You kill me to deny it. Farewell.

Bene. Tarry, sweet Beatrice.

268 even: *smooth, easy*

Beat. I am gone, though I am here: there is no love in you: nay, I pray you, let me go.

Bene. Beatrice,—

Beat. In faith, I will go.

Bene. We'll be friends first.

Beat. You dare easier be friends with me than fight with mine enemy.

Bene. Is Claudio thine enemy?

Beat. Is he not approved in the height a villain, that hath slandered, scorned, dishonoured my kinswoman? O! that I were a man. What! bear her in hand until they come to take hands, and then, with public accusation, uncovered slander, unmitigated rancour,—O God, that I were a man! I would eat his heart in the market-place.

Bene. Hear me, Beatrice,—

Beat. Talk with a man out at a window! a proper saying!

Bene. Nay, but Beatrice,—

Beat. Sweet Hero! she is wronged, she is slandered, she is undone.

Bene. Beat—

Beat. Princes and counties! Surely, a princely testimony, a goodly Count Comfect; a sweet gallant, surely! O! that I were a man for his sake, or that I had any friend would be a man for my sake! But manhood is melted into curtsies, valour into compliment, and men are only turned into tongue, and trim ones too: he is now as valiant as Hercules, that only tells a lie and swears it. I cannot be a man with wish-

298 gone: *absent in spirit*
306 height: *highest degree*
309 bear . . in hand: *delude*
310 uncovered: *open*
321 counties: *counts*
322 Comfect: *sweetmeat*

ing, therefore I will die a woman with grieving.

Bene. Tarry, good Beatrice. By this hand, I love thee.

Beat. Use it for my love some other way than swearing by it.

Bene. Think you in your soul the Count Claudio hath wronged Hero?

Beat. Yea, as sure as I have a thought or a soul.

Bene. Enough! I am engaged, I will challenge him. I will kiss your hand, and so leave you. By this hand, Claudio shall render me a dear account. As you hear of me, so think of me. Go, comfort your cousin: I must say she is dead; and so, farewell. [*Exeunt.*]

Scene Two

[*A Prison*]

Enter the Constables [*Dogberry and Verges*] *and the Town Clerk* [*Sexton*] *in gowns,* [*with the Watch, Conrade and*] *Borachio.*

Dogb. Is our whole dissembly appeared?

Verg. O! a stool and a cushion for the sexton.

Sexton. Which be the malefactors?

Dogb. Marry, that am I and my partner.

Verg. Nay, that's certain: we have the exhibition to examine.

Sexton. But which are the offenders that are to be examined? let them come before Master constable.

Sc. ii; *cf. n.* 1 dissembly: *i.e. assembly* 5 Dogb.; *cf. n.*
6 exhibition: *i.e. commission* (?)

Dogb. Yea, marry, let them come before me. What is your name, friend?

Bora. Borachio.

Dogb. Pray write down Borachio. Yours, sirrah?

Con. I am a gentleman, sir, and my name is Conrade.

Dogb. Write down Master gentleman Conrade. Masters, do you serve God?

Con.
Bora. } Yea, sir, we hope.

Dogb. Write down that they hope they serve God: and write God first; for God defend but God should go before such villains! Masters, it is proved already that you are little better than false knaves, and it will go near to be thought so shortly. How answer you for yourselves?

Con. Marry, sir, we say we are none.

Dogb. A marvellous witty fellow, I assure you; but I will go about with him. Come you hither, sirrah; a word in your ear: sir, I say to you, it is thought you are false knaves.

Bora. Sir, I say to you we are none.

Dogb. Well, stand aside. 'Fore God, they are both in a tale. Have you writ down, that they are none?

Sexton. Master constable, you go not the way to examine: you must call forth the watch that are their accusers.

Dogb. Yea, marry, that's the eftest way. Let the watch come forth. Masters, I charge you, in the prince's name, accuse these men.

25 go near to: *almost* 28 witty: *cunning*
29 go about with: *circumvent*
34 in a tale: *agreed on one story* 39 eftest: *quickest* (?)

First Watch. This man said, sir, that Don John, the prince's brother, was a villain.

Dogb. Write down Prince John a villain. Why, this is flat perjury, to call a prince's brother villain.

Bora. Master constable,—

Dogb. Pray thee, fellow, peace: I do not like thy look, I promise thee.

Sexton. What heard you him say else?

Sec. Watch. Marry, that he had received a thousand ducats of Don John for accusing the Lady Hero wrongfully.

Dogb. Flat burglary as ever was committed.

Verg. Yea, by the mass, that it is.

Sexton. What else, fellow?

First Watch. And that Count Claudio did mean, upon his words, to disgrace Hero before the whole assembly, and not marry her.

Dogb. O villain! thou wilt be condemned into everlasting redemption for this.

Sexton. What else?

Sec. Watch. This is all.

Sexton. And this is more, masters, than you can deny. Prince John is this morning secretly stolen away: Hero was in this manner accused, in this very manner refused, and, upon the grief of this, suddenly died. Master constable, let these men be bound, and brought to Leonato's: I will go before and show him their examination. [*Exit.*]

Dogb. Come, let them be opinioned.

Verg. Let them be in the hands—

Con. Off, coxcomb!

72 opinioned: *i.e. pinioned* 73, 74 *Cf. n.*

Dogb. God's my life! where's the sexton? let him write down the prince's officer coxcomb. Come, bind them. Thou naughty varlet! 77

Con. Away! you are an ass; you are an ass.

Dogb. Dost thou not suspect my place? Dost thou not suspect my years? O that he were here to write me down an ass! but, masters, remember that I am an ass; though it be not written down, yet forget not that I am an ass. No, thou villain, thou art full of piety, as shall be proved upon thee by good witness. I am a wise fellow; and, which is more, an officer; and, which is more, a householder; and, which is more, as pretty a piece of flesh as any in Messina; and one that knows the law, go to; and a rich fellow enough, go to; and a fellow that hath had losses; and one that hath two gowns, and everything handsome about him. Bring him away. O that I had been writ down an ass! 93

Exeunt.

ACT FIFTH

Scene One

[*Before Leonato's House.*]

Enter Leonato and his brother [*Antonio*].

Ant. If you go on thus, you will kill yourself;
And 'tis not wisdom thus to second grief
Against yourself.

Leon. I pray thee, cease thy counsel,

77 naughty: *good-for-naught*
79 suspect: *i.e. respect*
84 piety: *i.e. impiety*
87 householder: *head of a household*
88 as pretty . . flesh: *as fine a fellow*
2 second: *assist*

Which falls into mine ears as profitless
As water in a sieve: give not me counsel;
Nor let no comforter delight mine ear
But such a one whose wrongs do suit with mine:
Bring me a father that so lov'd his child,
Whose joy of her is overwhelm'd like mine,
And bid him speak of patience;
Measure his woe the length and breadth of mine,
And let it answer every strain for strain,
As thus for thus and such a grief for such,
In every lineament, branch, shape, and form:
If such a one will smile, and stroke his beard;
Bid sorrow wag, cry 'hem' when he should groan,
Patch grief with proverbs; make misfortune drunk
With candle-wasters; bring him yet to me,
And I of him will gather patience.
But there is no such man; for, brother, men
Can counsel and speak comfort to that grief
Which they themselves not feel; but, tasting it,
Their counsel turns to passion, which before
Would give preceptial medicine to rage,
Fetter strong madness in a silken thread,
Charm ache with air and agony with words.
No, no; 'tis all men's office to speak patience
To those that wring under the load of sorrow,
But no man's virtue nor sufficiency
To be so moral when he shall endure
The like himself. Therefore give me no counsel:
My griefs cry louder than advertisement.

7 suit: *agree* 12 strain: *strong feeling* 16 wag: *pass on; cf. n.*
18 candle-wasters: *sleepless revellers or students*
24 preceptial: *made up of precepts*
26 air: *mere breath* 28 wring: *writhe*
30 moral: *full of wisdom* 32 advertisement: *advice*

Ant. Therein do men from children nothing differ.
Leon. I pray thee, peace! I will be flesh and blood;
For there was never yet philosopher
That could endure the toothache patiently,
However they have writ the style of gods
And made a push at chance and sufferance.
Ant. Yet bend not all the harm upon yourself;
Make those that do offend you suffer too.
Leon. There thou speak'st reason: nay, I will do so.
My soul doth tell me Hero is belied;
And that shall Claudio know; so shall the prince,
And all of them that thus dishonour her.
Ant. Here come the prince and Claudic hastily.

Enter Prince and Claudio.

D. Pedro. Good den, good den.
Claud. Good day to both of you.
Leon. Hear you, my lords,—
D. Pedro. We have some haste, Leonato.
Leon. Some haste, my lord! well, fare you well, my lord:
Are you so hasty now?—well, all is one.
D. Pedro. Nay, do not quarrel with us, good old man.
Ant. If he could right himself with quarrelling,

37 style of: *language worthy of*
38 push; *cf. n.* sufferance: *suffering*
49 all is one: *'tis all the same*

Some of us would lie low.
Claud. Who wrongs him?
Leon. Marry, thou dost wrong me; thou dissembler, thou.
Nay, never lay thy hand upon thy sword;
I fear thee not.
Claud. Marry, beshrew my hand,
If it should give your age such case of fear.
In faith, my hand meant nothing to my sword.
Leon. Tush, tush, man! never fleer and jest at me:
I speak not like a dotard nor a fool,
As, under privilege of age, to brag
What I have done being young, or what would do,
Were I not old. Know, Claudio, to thy head,
Thou hast so wrong'd mine innocent child and me
That I am forc'd to lay my reverence by,
And, with grey hairs and bruise of many days,
Do challenge thee to trial of a man.
I say thou hast belied mine innocent child:
Thy slander hath gone through and through her heart,
And she lies buried with her ancestors;
O! in a tomb where never scandal slept,
Save this of hers, fram'd by thy villainy!
Claud. My villainy?
Leon. Thine, Claudio; thine, I say.
D. Pedro. You say not right, old man.
Leon. My lord, my lord,
I'll prove it on his body, if he dare,
Despite his nice fence and his active practice,
His May of youth and bloom of lustihood.

55 beshrew: *curse* 58 fleer: *sneer*
62 to thy head: *to thy face* 75 fence: *skill in fencing*
76 lustihood: *vigor*

Claud. Away! I will not have to do with you.
Leon. Canst thou so daff me? Thou hast kill'd my child;
If thou kill'st me, boy, thou shalt kill a man.
Ant. He shall kill two of us, and men indeed:
But that's no matter; let him kill one first:
Win me and wear me; let him answer me.
Come, follow me, boy; come, sir boy, come, follow me.
Sir boy, I'll whip you from your foining fence;
Nay, as I am a gentleman, I will.
Leon. Brother,—
Ant. Content yourself. God knows I lov'd my niece;
And she is dead, slander'd to death by villains,
That dare as well answer a man indeed
As I dare take a serpent by the tongue.
Boys, apes, braggarts, Jacks, milksops!
Leon. Brother Antony,—
Ant. Hold you content. What, man! I know them, yea,
And what they weigh, even to the utmost scruple,
Scambling, out-facing, fashion-monging boys,
That lie and cog and flout, deprave and slander,
Go anticly, show outward hideousness,
And speak off half a dozen dangerous words,
How they might hurt their enemies, if they durst;
And this is all!
Leon. But, brother Antony,—
Ant. Come, 'tis no matter:

82 Win me, *etc.; cf. n.*
84 foining: *thrusting*
94 Scambling: *contentious* out-facing: *swaggering*
95 cog: *cheat* deprave: *vilify*
96 anticly: *dressed like clowns*

Do not you meddle, let me deal in this.

D. Pedro. Gentlemen both, we will not wake your patience.
My heart is sorry for your daughter's death;
But, on my honour, she was charg'd with nothing
But what was true and very full of proof.

Leon. My lord, my lord—

D. Pedro. I will not hear you.

Leon. No?
Come, brother, away. I will be heard.—

Ant. And shall, or some of us will smart for it. *Exeunt Leonato and Antonio.*

Enter Benedick.

D. Pedro. See, see; here comes the man we went to seek.

Claud. Now, signior, what news?

Bene. Good day, my lord.

D. Pedro. Welcome, signior: you are almost come to part almost a fray.

Claud. We had like to have had our two noses snapped off with two old men without teeth.

D. Pedro. Leonato and his brother. What thinkest thou? Had we fought, I doubt we should have been too young for them.

Bene. In a false quarrel there is no true valour. I came to seek you both.

Claud. We have been up and down to seek thee; for we are high-proof melancholy, and would fain have it beaten away. Wilt thou use thy wit?

102 wake your patience; *cf. n.*
124 high-proof: *in the highest degree*

Bene. It is in my scabbard; shall I draw it?

D. Pedro. Dost thou wear thy wit by thy side?

Claud. Never any did so, though very many have been beside their wit. I will bid thee draw, as we do the minstrels; draw, to pleasure us.

D. Pedro. As I am an honest man, he looks pale. Art thou sick, or angry?

Claud. What, courage, man! What though care killed a cat, thou hast mettle enough in thee to kill care.

Bene. Sir, I shall meet your wit in the career, an you charge it against me. I pray you choose another subject.

Claud. Nay then, give him another staff: this last was broke cross.

D. Pedro. By this light, he changes more and more: I think he be angry indeed.

Claud. If he be, he knows how to turn his girdle.

Bene. Shall I speak a word in your ear?

Claud. God bless me from a challenge!

Bene. [*Aside to Claudio.*] You are a villain; I jest not: I will make it good how you dare, with what you dare, and when you dare. Do me right, or I will protest your cowardice. You have killed a sweet lady, and her death shall fall heavy on you. Let me hear from you.

Claud. Well I will meet you, so I may have good cheer.

D. Pedro. What, a feast, a feast?

131 beside their wit: *out of their wits* draw; *cf. n.*
138 in the career: *at full speed*
139 charge: *direct* 141 staff: *lance* 142 broke cross; *cf. n.*
145 turn his girdle; *cf. n.*
151 Do me right: *give me satisfaction* 152 protest: *proclaim*

Claud. I' faith, I thank him; he hath bid me to a calf's-head and a capon, the which if I do not carve most curiously, say my knife's naught. Shall I not find a woodcock too? 161

Bene. Sir, your wit ambles well; it goes easily.

D. Pedro. I'll tell thee how Beatrice praised thy wit the other day. I said, thou hadst a fine wit. 'True,' says she, 'a fine little one.' 'No,' said I, 'a great wit.' 'Right,' said she, 'a great gross one.' 'Nay,' said I, 'a good wit.' 'Just,' said she, 'it hurts nobody.' Nay,' said I, 'the gentlemen is wise.' 'Certain,' said she, 'a wise gentleman.' 'Nay,' said I, 'he hath the tongues.' 'That I believe,' said she, 'for he swore a thing to me on Monday night, which he forswore on Tuesday morning: there's a double tongue; there's two tongues.' Thus did she, an hour together, trans-shape thy particular virtues; yet at last she concluded with a sigh, thou wast the properest man in Italy. 178

Claud. For the which she wept heartily and said she cared not.

D. Pedro. Yea, that she did; but yet, for all that, an if she did not hate him deadly, she would love him dearly. The old man's daughter told us all. 184

Claud. All, all; and moreover, God saw him when he was hid in the garden.

D. Pedro. But when shall we set the savage bull's horns on the sensible Benedick's head? 189

160 curiously: *daintily* naught: *worthless*
161 woodcock: *a stupid bird*
170 a wise gentleman; *cf. n.* 176 trans-shape: *distort*

Claud. Yea, and text underneath, 'Here dwells Benedick the married man!'

Bene. Fare you well, boy: you know my mind. I will leave you now to your gossip-like humour: you break jests as braggarts do their blades, which, God be thanked, hurt not. My lord, for your many courtesies I thank you: I must discontinue your company. Your brother the bastard is fled from Messina: you have, among you, killed a sweet and innocent lady. For my Lord Lack-beard there, he and I shall meet; and till then, peace be with him. [*Exit.*]

D. Pedro. He is in earnest.

Claud. In most profound earnest; and, I'll warrant you, for the love of Beatrice.

D. Pedro. And hath challenged thee?

Claud. Most sincerely.

D. Pedro. What a pretty thing man is when he goes in his doublet and hose and leaves off his wit!

Claud. He is then a giant to an ape; but then is an ape a doctor to such a man.

D. Pedro. But, soft you; let me be: pluck up, my heart, and be sad! Did he not say my brother was fled?

Enter Constable [Dogberry, Verges, and Watch, with] Conrade and Borachio.

Dogb. Come, you, sir: if justice cannot tame you, she shall ne'er weigh more reasons in her balance. Nay, an you be a cursing hypocrite once, you must be looked to.

208 leaves off his wit; *cf. n.* 211 doctor: *learned man; cf.*
212 soft you: *gently!* pluck up: *rouse thyself*

D. Pedro. How now! two of my brother's men bound! Borachio, one!

Claud. Hearken after their offence, my lord.

D. Pedro. Officers, what offence have these men done?

Dogb. Marry, sir, they have committed false report; moreover, they have spoken untruths; secondarily, they are slanders; sixth and lastly, they have belied a lady; thirdly, they have verified unjust things; and to conclude, they are lying knaves.

D. Pedro. First, I ask thee what they have done; thirdly, I ask thee what's their offence; sixth and lastly, why they are committed; and, to conclude, what you lay to their charge?

Claud. Rightly reasoned, and in his own division; and, by my troth, there's one meaning well suited.

D. Pedro. Who have you offended, masters, that you are thus bound to your answer? this learned constable is too cunning to be understood. What's your offence?

Bora. Sweet prince, let me go no further to mine answer: do you hear me, and let this count kill me. I have deceived even your very eyes: what your wisdoms could not discover, these shallow fools have brought to light; who in the night overheard me confessing to this man how Don John your brother incensed me to slander the Lady Hero; how you were brought into the orchard and saw me court Margaret

21 Hearken after: *inquire into*
8 verified: *i.e. testified*
38 to your answer: *to answer for your conduct*
47 incensed: *instigated*
226 slanders: *i.e. slanderers*
236 well suited; *cf. n.*

in Hero's garments; how you disgraced her, when you should marry her. My villainy they have upon record; which I had rather seal with my death than repeat over to my shame. The lady is dead upon mine and my master's false accusation; and, briefly, I desire nothing but the reward of a villain.

D. Pedro. Runs not this speech like iron through your blood?

Claud. I have drunk poison whiles he utter'd it.

D. Pedro. But did my brother set thee on to this?

Bora. Yea; and paid me richly for the practice of it.

D. Pedro. He is compos'd and fram'd of treachery:
And fled he is upon this villainy.

Claud. Sweet Hero! now thy image doth appear
In the rare semblance that I lov'd it first.

Dogb. Come, bring away the plaintiffs: by this time our sexton hath reformed Signior Leonato of the matter. And masters, do not forget to specify, when time and place shall serve, that I am an ass.

Verg. Here, here comes Master Signior Leonato, and the sexton too.

Enter Leonato [, Antonio, and the Sexton].

Leon. Which is the villain? Let me see his eyes,

265 plaintiffs: *i.e. defendants* 266 reformed: *i.e. informed*
268 specify: *i.e. testify* (?)

That, when I note another man like him,
I may avoid him. Which of these is he?
Bora. If you would know your wronger, look on me.
Leon. Art thou the slave that with thy breath hast kill'd
Mine innocent child?
Bora. Yea, even I alone.
Leon. No, not so, villain; thou beliest thyself:
Here stand a pair of honourable men;
A third is fled, that had a hand in it.
I thank you, princes, for my daughter's death:
Record it with your high and worthy deeds.
'Twas bravely done, if you bethink you of it.
Claud. I know not how to pray your patience;
Yet I must speak. Choose your revenge yourself;
Impose me to what penance your invention
Can lay upon my sin: yet sinn'd I not
But in mistaking.
D. Pedro. By my soul, nor I:
And yet, to satisfy this good old man,
I would bend under any heavy weight
That he'll enjoin me to.
Leon. I cannot bid you bid my daughter live;
That were impossible: but, I pray you both,
Possess the people in Messina here
How innocent she died; and if your love
Can labour aught in sad invention,
Hang her an epitaph upon her tomb,

286 Impose: *subject* 294 Possess: *inform*

And sing it to her bones: sing it to-night.
To-morrow morning come you to my house,
And since you could not be my son-in-law,
Be yet my nephew. My brother hath a daughter,
Almost the copy of my child that's dead,
And she alone is heir to both of us:
Give her the right you should have given her cousin,
And so dies my revenge.

Claud. O noble sir,
Your over-kindness doth wring tears from me!
I do embrace your offer; and dispose
For henceforth of poor Claudio.

Leon. To-morrow then I will expect your coming;
To-night I take my leave. This naughty man
Shall face to face be brought to Margaret,
Who, I believe, was pack'd in all this wrong,
Hir'd to it by your brother.

Bora. No, by my soul she was not;
Nor knew not what she did when she spoke to me;
But always hath been just and virtuous
In anything that I do know by her.

Dogb. Moreover, sir,—which, indeed, is not under white and black,—this plaintiff here, the offender, did call me ass: I beseech you, let it be remembered in his punishment. And also, the watch heard them talk of one Deformed: they say he wears a key in his ear and a lock hanging by it, and borrows money in God's name, the which he hath used so long and never

312 pack'd: *implicated*
316 by: *concerning*
318 under black and white: *in writing*

paid, that now men grow hard-hearted, and will lend nothing for God's sake. Pray you, examine him upon that point.

Leon. I thank thee for thy care and honest pains.

Dogb. Your worship speaks like a most thankful and reverend youth, and I praise God for you.

Leon. There's for thy pains.

Dogb. God save the foundation!

Leon. Go, I discharge thee of thy prisoner, and I thank thee.

Dogb. I leave an arrant knave with your worship; which I beseech your worship to correct yourself, for the example of others. God keep your worship! I wish your worship well; God restore you to health! I humbly give you leave to depart, and if a merry meeting may be wished, God prohibit it! Come, neighbour.

Exeunt [*Dogberry and Verges*].

Leon. Until to-morrow morning, lords, farewell.
Ant. Farewell, my lords: we look for you to-morrow.
D. Pedro. We will not fail.
Claud. To-night I'll mourn with Hero.
[*Exeunt Don Pedro and Claudio.*]
Leon. [*To the Watch.*] Bring you these fellows on. We'll talk with Margaret,
How her acquaintance grew with this lewd fellow. *Exeunt.*

334 foundation; *cf. n.* 343 prohibit: *i.e. permit* (?)

Scene Two

[*Leonato's Orchard.*]

Enter Benedick and Margaret.

Bene. Pray thee, sweet Mistress Margaret, deserve well at my hands by helping me to the speech of Beatrice.

Marg. Will you then write me a sonnet in praise of my beauty?

Bene. In so high a style, Margaret, that no man living shall come over it; for, in most comely truth, thou deservest it.

Marg. To have no man come over me! why, shall I always keep below stairs?

Bene. Thy wit is as quick as the greyhound's mouth; it catches.

Marg. And yours as blunt as the fencer's foils, which hit, but hurt not.

Bene. A most manly wit, Margaret; it will not hurt a woman: and so, I pray thee, call Beatrice. I give thee the bucklers.

Marg. Give us the swords, we have bucklers of our own.

Bene. If you use them, Margaret, you must put in the pikes with a vice; and they are dangerous weapons for maids.

Marg. Well, I will call Beatrice to you, who I think hath legs.

Bene. And therefore will come.

Exit Margaret.

6 style; *cf. n.* 10 keep below stairs: *remain a servant*
17 give . . bucklers: *yield* 21 vice; *cf. n.*

'The god of love,
That sits above,
And knows me, and knows me, 28
How pitiful I deserve,—'

I mean, in singing; but in loving, Leander the good swimmer, Troilus the first employer of pandars, and a whole book full of these quondam carpet-mongers, whose names yet run smoothly in the even road of a blank verse, why, they were never so truly turned over and over as my poor self, in love. Marry, I cannot show it in rime; I have tried: I can find out no rime to 'lady' but 'baby,' an innocent rime; for 'scorn,' 'horn,' a hard rime; for 'school,' 'fool,' a babbling rime; very ominous endings: no, I was not born under a riming planet, nor I cannot woo in festival terms. 42

Enter Beatrice.

Sweet Beatrice, wouldst thou come when I called thee?

Beat. Yea, signior; and depart when you bid me.

Bene. O, stay but till then! 47

Beat. 'Then' is spoken; fare you well now: and yet, ere I go, let me go with that I came for; which is, with knowing what hath passed between you and Claudio. 51

Bene. Only foul words; and thereupon I will kiss thee.

Beat. Foul words is but foul wind, and foul

30, 31 Leander . . Troilus: *cf. n.*
32 quondam carpet-mongers: *carpet-knights of old*
38 innocent: *silly* 41 riming planet: *cf. n.*
42 festival terms: *language not used every day*

wind is but foul breath, and foul breath is noisome; therefore I will depart unkissed.

Bene. Thou hast frighted the word out of his right sense, so forcible is thy wit. But I must tell thee plainly, Claudio undergoes my challenge, and either I must shortly hear from him, or I will subscribe him a coward. And, I pray thee now, tell me, for which of my bad parts didst thou first fall in love with me?

Beat. For them all together; which maintained so politic a state of evil that they will not admit any good part to intermingle with them. But for which of my good parts did you first suffer love for me?

Bene. 'Suffer love,' a good epithet! I do suffer love indeed, for I love thee against my will.

Beat. In spite of your heart, I think. Alas, poor heart! If you spite it for my sake, I will spite it for yours; for I will never love that which my friend hates.

Bene. Thou and I are too wise to woo peaceably.

Beat. It appears not in this confession: there's not one wise man among twenty that will praise himself.

Bene. An old, an old instance, Beatrice, that lived in the time of good neighbours. If a man do not erect in this age his own tomb ere he dies, he shall live no longer in monument than the bell rings and the widow weeps.

57 his: *its*
59 undergoes: *is subject to* (?)
61 subscribe: *write down*
65 politic: *prudently governed*
81 instance: *saying* (?)
82 time of good neighbours; *cf. n.*

Beat. And how long is that, think you?

Bene. Question: why, an hour in clamour and a quarter in rheum: therefore it is most expedient for the wise,—if Don Worm, his conscience, find no impediment to the contrary,—to be the trumpet of his own virtues, as I am to myself. So much for praising myself, who, I myself will bear witness, is praiseworthy. And now tell me, how doth your cousin?

Beat. Very ill.

Bene. And how do you?

Beat. Very ill too.

Bene. Serve God, love me, and mend. There will I leave you too, for here comes one in haste.

Enter Ursula.

Urs. Madam, you must come to your uncle. Yonder's old coil at home: it is proved, my Lady Hero hath been falsely accused, the prince and Claudio mightily abused; and Don John is the author of all, who is fled and gone. Will you come presently?

Beat. Will you go hear this news, signior?

Bene. I will live in thy heart, die in thy lap, and be buried in thy eyes; and moreover I will go with thee to thy uncle's. *Exeunt.*

87 Question: *that is the question* clamour: *i.e. sound of the bell*
88 rheum: *tears*
89 Don Worm; *cf. n.*
98 mend: *recover health*
102 old coil: *a great ado*
104 abused: *deceived*

Scene Three

[*Within the Church*]

Enter Claudio, Prince, and three or four with tapers.

Claud. Is this the monument of Leonato?

A Lord. It is, my lord.

[*Claud., reading the*] *Epitaph.*

Done to death by slanderous tongues
  Was the Hero that here lies:
Death, in guerdon of her wrongs,
  Gives her fame which never dies.
So the life that died with shame
Lives in death with glorious fame.'

Hang thou there upon the tomb,
Praising her when I am dumb.
Now, music, sound, and sing your solemn hymn.

Song.

'Pardon, goddess of the night,
Those that slew thy virgin knight;
For the which, with songs of woe,
Round about her tomb they go.
  Midnight, assist our moan;
  Help us to sigh and groan,
  Heavily, heavily:
  Graves, yawn and yield your dead,
  Till death be uttered,
    Heavily, heavily.'

Claud. Now, unto thy bones good night!
  Yearly will I do this rite.

9, 10 *Cf. n.* 20 uttered; *cf. n.*

D. Pedro. Good morrow, masters: put your torches out.
The wolves have prey'd; and look, the gentle day,
Before the wheels of Phœbus, round about
Dapples the drowsy east with spots of grey.
Thanks to you all, and leave us: fare you well.
Claud. Good morrow, masters: each his several way.
D. Pedro. Come, let us hence, and put on other weeds;
And then to Leonato's we will go.
Claud. And Hymen now with luckier issue speed's,
Than this for whom we render'd up this woe!
Exeunt.

Scene Four

[*Leonato's House*]

Enter Leonato, Antonio, Benedick, [Beatrice,] Margaret, Ursula, Friar and Hero.

Friar. Did I not tell you she was innocent?
Leon. So are the prince and Claudio, who accus'd her
Upon the error that you heard debated:
But Margaret was in some fault for this,
Although against her will, as it appears
In the true course of all the question.
Ant. Well, I am glad that all things sort so well.

25 have prey'd: *have ceased to prey (night is over)*
30 weeds: *garments*
32 luckier issue: *better fortune* speed's: *grant us help*
33 this; *cf. n.*
3 debated: *discussed* 6 In the true course, *etc.: cf. n.*

Bene. And so am I, being else by faith enforc'd
To call young Claudio to a reckoning for it.
Leon. Well, daughter, and you gentlewomen all,
Withdraw into a chamber by yourselves,
And when I send for you, come hither, mask'd:
The prince and Claudio promis'd by this hour
To visit me. *Exeunt ladies.*
You know your office, brother;
You must be father to your brother's daughter,
And give her to young Claudio.
Ant. Which I will do with confirm'd countenance.
Bene. Friar, I must entreat your pains, I think.
Friar. To do what, signior?
Bene. To bind me, or undo me; one of them.
Signior Leonato, truth it is, good signior,
Your niece regards me with an eye of favour.
Leon. That eye my daughter lent her: 'tis most true.
Bene. And I do with an eye of love requite her.
Leon. The sight whereof I think, you had from me,
From Claudio, and the prince. But what's your will?
Bene. Your answer, sir, is enigmatical:
But, for my will, my will is your good will
May stand with ours, this day to be conjoin'd
In the state of honourable marriage:
In which, good friar, I shall desire your help.
Leon. My heart is with your liking.
Friar. And my help.
Here come the prince and Claudio.

8 by faith: *by my pledged word*
17 confirm'd: *steady*
20 undo: (1) *unbind,* (2) *ruin*

Enter Prince and Claudio, with Attendants.

D. Pedro. Good morrow to this fair assembly.

Leon. Good morrow, prince; good morrow, Claudio:
We here attend you. Are you yet determin'd
To-day to marry with my brother's daughter?

Claud. I'll hold my mind, were she an Ethiop.

Leon. Call her forth, brother: here's the friar ready. [*Exit Antonio.*]

D. Pedro. Good morrow, Benedick. Why, what's the matter,
That you have such a February face,
So full of frost, of storm and cloudiness?

Claud. I think he thinks upon the savage bull.
Tush! fear not, man, we'll tip thy horns with gold,
And all Europa shall rejoice at thee,
As once Europa did at lusty Jove,
When he would play the noble beast in love.

Bene. Bull Jove, sir, had an amiable low:
And some such strange bull leap'd your father's cow,
And got a calf in that same noble feat,
Much like to you, for you have just his bleat.

Claud. For this I owe you: here come other reckonings.

Enter Antonio [with] Hero, Beatrice, Margaret, Ursula [masked].

Which is the lady I must seize upon?

Ant. This same is she, and I do give you her.

Claud. Why, then she's mine. Sweet, let me see your face.

43 *Cf. n.*
45, 46 Europa; *cf. n.*
52 owe you: *i.e. owe you an answer*

Leon. No, that you shall not, till you take her hand
Before this friar, and swear to marry her.
Claud. Give me your hand: before this holy friar,
I am your husband, if you like of me.
Hero. And when I liv'd, I was your other wife:
[*Unmasking.*]
And when you lov'd, you were my other husband.
Claud. Another Hero!
Hero. Nothing certainer
One Hero died defil'd, but I do live,
And surely as I live, I am a maid.
D.Pedro. The former Hero! Hero that is dead!
Leon. She died, my lord, but whiles her slander liv'd.
Friar. All this amazement can I qualify:
When after that the holy rites are ended,
I'll tell you largely of fair Hero's death:
Meantime, let wonder seem familiar,
And to the chapel let us presently.
Bene. Soft and fair, friar. Which is Beatrice?
Beat. [*Unmasking.*] I answer to that name. What is your will?
Bene. Do not you love me?
Beat. Why, no; no more than reason.
Bene. Why, then, your uncle and the prince and Claudio
Have been deceived; for they swore you did.
Beat. Do not you love me?
Bene. Troth, no; no more than reason.

59 like of: *care for* 67 qualify: *moderate* 69 largely: *fully*
70 let wonder, *etc.; cf. n.* 77 Troth: *by my troth*

Beat. Why, then, my cousin, Margaret, and Ursula,
Are much deceiv'd; for they did swear you did.
Bene. They swore that you were almost sick for me.
Beat. They swore that you were well-nigh dead for me.
Bene. 'Tis no such matter. Then, you do not love me?
Beat. No, truly, but in friendly recompense.
Leon. Come, cousin, I am sure you love the gentleman.
Claud. And I'll be sworn upon 't that he loves her;
For here's a paper written in his hand,
A halting sonnet of his own pure brain,
Fashion'd to Beatrice.
Hero. And here's another,
Writ in my cousin's hand, stolen from her pocket,
Containing her affection unto Benedick.

Bene. A miracle! here's our own hands against our hearts. Come, I will have thee; but, by this light, I take thee for pity.

Beat. I would not deny you; but, by this good day, I yield upon great persuasion, and partly to save your life, for I was told you were in a consumption.

Bene. Peace! I will stop your mouth. [*Kisses her.*]

D. Pedro. How dost thou, 'Benedick, the married man'?

Bene. I'll tell thee what, prince; a college of

87 his own pure: *purely his own*   99, 100 *Cf n.*

witcrackers cannot flout me out of my humour. Dost thou think I care for a satire or an epigram? No; if a man will be beaten with brains, a' shall wear nothing handsome about him. In brief, since I do purpose to marry, I will think nothing to any purpose that the world can say against it; and therefore never flout at me for what I have said against it, for man is a giddy thing, and this is my conclusion. For thy part, Claudio, I did think to have beaten thee; but, in that thou art like to be my kinsman, live unbruised, and love my cousin.

Claud. I had well hoped thou wouldst have denied Beatrice, that I might have cudgelled thee out of thy single life, to make thee a double-dealer; which, out of question, thou wilt be, if my cousin do not look exceeding narrowly to thee.

Bene. Come, come, we are friends. Let's have a dance ere we are married, that we may lighten our own hearts and our wives' heels.

Leon. We'll have dancing afterward.

Bene. First, of my word; therefore play, music! Prince, thou art sad; get thee a wife, get thee a wife: there is no staff more reverend than one tipped with horn.

Enter Messenger.

Mes. My lord, your brother John is ta'en in flight,
And brought with armed men back to Messina.

104 beaten with brains, *etc.; cf. n.*
116 double-dealer; *cf. n.*
124 of: *on*

Bene. Think not on him till to-morrow: I'll devise thee brave punishments for him. Strike up, pipers! *Dance.*

131 brave: *fine*

FINIS.

NOTES

I. i. S. d. [*Before Antonio's Orchard*]. etc. The quarto edition of this play (1600) makes no division into either acts or scenes. The folio edition (1623) divides the acts correctly, but does not mark the separate scenes, except in the case of the present one, the first. Neither of the early editions indicates where the action of the various scenes occurs. In the present instance modern editors have usually located the scene 'Before Leonato's House.' Lines 98-100 and 286, however, suggest that Leonato and his family have come to meet their distinguished guests near the edge of the town, and lines 10-12 of scene ii point to the neighborhood of Antonio's orchard (*i.e.* garden) as the place of meeting. See L. Mason, *Modern Philology*, xi. 379-89.

I. i. S. d. *Innogen, his wife.* Leonato's wife is mentioned only in this stage direction and in that at the opening of Act II. Modern editors have therefore regularly omitted her name in both places. It is possible that Shakespeare gave her a small part in the first draft of the play, and subsequently cut it out for the sake of compression.

I. i. 7 *sort.* The interpretation of this word given in the footnote is preferred by most editors; but it is possible to take the word in the more general sense which it bears at present: 'kind.'

I. i. 30 *Mountanto.* A term in fencing, 'upper-cut,' used by Beatrice to characterize Benedick's lively and pugnacious disposition.

I. i. 40-42 *challenged Cupid . . bird-bolt.* The jest is that Benedick vaingloriously challenged Cupid to a contest at shooting hearts, to which Leonato's fool replied by suggesting himself as Benedick's proper competitor and the childish bird-bolt as his proper weapon.

I. i. 60 *stuffed . . stuffing.* Beatrice calls Benedick a 'stuffed' man because of his proneness to over-eat; then, playing with the phrase, suggests that his 'stuffing'—what is in him, what he is made of—is of no very fine quality.

I. i. 67 *five wits.* 'Not the five senses, but the five other wits: the memory, fantasy, estimation, imagination, and common wit. Benedick is left the last only.'

I. i. 70 *bear it for a difference.* Alluding to a term in heraldry, where a 'difference' was some slight mark added to differentiate coats of arms otherwise indistinguishable.

I. i. 72 *to be known,* etc. This infinitive clause is the subject of the sentence. Bare recognition as a rational creature, not a dumb animal, is all the intellectual wealth Benedick has left.

I. i. 90 *the Benedick.* Beatrice affects to think the harmful result of Benedick's company a physical disease, like the colic.

I. i. 142 *a predestinate scratched face.* The gentleman destined to marry Beatrice is predestined to have his face scratched by her. If she refuses to marry, he will escape that destiny.

I. i. 143 *an.* The conjunction 'and,' one old meaning of which was 'if.' Here and regularly elsewhere the old editions spell 'and,' which modern editors alter for the sake of clearness.

I. i. 146 *A bird of my tongue,* etc. 'A bird taught to speak like me,' alluding to Benedick's gibe, 'parrot-teacher.' The latter part of the sentence implies that only a beast could be taught to speak like Benedick.

I. i. 151 *a jade's trick.* Some such trick of a bad horse as slipping the head out of the collar and escaping. Beatrice gibes at Benedick's sudden breaking off of the dispute.

I. i. 171 *noted.* Benedick puns on one of the less obvious meanings of the word. Possibly the sense he has in mind is to provide with notes, set to music: 'I did not set the young lady to music,' *i.e.* did not go into raptures over her.

I. i. 192, 193 *Cupid . . carpenter.* It would be an obvious absurdity to select the blind god, Cupid, to spy out the sitting hare, or to name Vulcan, the god of the flaming forge, as a proper person to work with the carpenter's inflammable materials.

I. i. 208 *wear his cap with suspicion.* 'Deceived husbands, according to the ancient jest, wore invisible horns. Every husband, therefore, would suspect his cap of concealing horns.' (MacCracken.)

I. i. 212 *sigh away Sundays.* It is hardly clear whether Sundays are particularly named because the days normally most happily spent or because the discontented husband would be most conscious of his yoke in the special domesticity of Sundays.

I. i. 226-228 *Like the old tale,* etc. An old children's tale, somewhat similar to that of Bluebeard, survived till the eighteenth century, in which occurred the words: 'It is not so, nor it was not so, and God forbid it should be so.'

I. i. 251 *recheat winded in my forehead . . invisible baldrick.* Another allusion to the invisible 'horns'; cf. note on l. 208. The recheat was a horn blast blown (*winded*) to recall the hounds from the chase; the baldrick, a strap worn across the shoulder and supporting the horn.

I. i. 264 *for the sign of blind Cupid.* Alluding to the pictorial signs hung up before places of business in Shakespeare's time. Benedick, treated as he suggests and hung up at the door, would make a proper illustration for 'The Blind Cupid.'

I. i. 267 *hang me in a bottle like a cat,* etc. 'Bottle' means probably the wicker basket used to hold the cat used as the mark in archery contests.

I. i. 269 *called Adam.* A special title of honor for the successful archer, doubtless from the fame of the archer-outlaw of the ballads, Adam Bell.

I. i. 271 *'In time the savage bull doth bear the yoke.'* A line quoted from memory, and not quite accurately, from Thomas Kyd's famous *Spanish Tragedy* (composed about 1587).

I. i. 281, 282 *Cupid . . Venice.* Venice was famed for frivolity.

I. i. 284 *temporize.* The meaning is not certain. 'Come to terms' is one explanation; another, rather more probable, is 'become tempered', *i.e.* grow milder. 'With the hours' means 'in the course of time.'

I. i. 290-294 *and so I commit you . . your loving friend, Benedick.* The words of Benedick suggest to Claudio the conventional mode of concluding formal letters, which he and Don Pedro proceed to parody. The sixth of July, formerly celebrated as Midsummer Day, is mentioned because of its suggestion of 'midsummer madness.'

I. i. 296 *guarded with fragments,* etc. Metaphors from tailoring. Benedick means that Don

Pedro and Claudio cannot in conscience afford to mock at trite phrases ('flout old ends'), for their own conversation is often made up of just such materials very poorly assimilated.

I. i. 327 *The fairest grant is the necessity.* The best gift is the one which just fits the need of the recipient; *i.e.* it is a mistake to be excessive.

I. ii. 2 *my cousin, your son.* Antonio's son is not elsewhere mentioned, and V. i. 303 suggests that he has no son. The inconsistency may be due to oversight. The 'cousins' and 'cousin' addressed by Leonato in ll. 27 and 29 are probably more distant relatives, dependants of his household.

I. iii. 12 *born under Saturn.* According to the old belief, persons born under the domination of the planet Saturn acquired the morose disposition hence called *saturnine.*

I. iii. 61 *smoking a musty room.* Elizabethan rooms, strewn with stale rushes, often required perfuming in order to dispel unpleasant odors.

comes me. Shakespeare very frequently employs a dative personal pronoun, as here, in a sense not found in modern usage. It is sometimes called the 'ethical' dative and merely suggests the interest of the person referred to in the act mentioned.

II. i. 43 *lead his apes into hell.* An allusion to a very common ancient saying that women who died old maids 'led apes in hell.' The origin of the phrase is uncertain; it may refer to the weakness of elderly spinsters for pet animals. Small apes held the place in their affection in Tudor times which cats hold to-day.

II. i. 51 *for the heavens.* The phrase can be interpreted either (1) 'on my way to heaven,'

St. Peter being the gate-keeper whom one met before entering; or (2) as a petty oath equivalent to 'by heaven' or perhaps 'for dear life.'

II. i. 86 *I can see a church by daylight.* 'I am not wholly blind.' The church would be the most conspicuous object in nearly any old town.

II. i. 100 *Philemon's roof.* A reference to the story in Ovid's *Metamorphoses* (bk. viii) of how the peasant couple, Philemon and Baucis, entertained Jupiter under their humble roof. Hence, *thatch'd* in line 103, peasant cottages having thatched roofs.

II. i. 115 *Answer, clerk.* Balthazar's *Amen* in the previous speech reminds Margaret of the parish clerk, whose business was to read out the responses at church in a loud voice.

II. i. 137 *the 'Hundred Merry Tales.'* A popular collection of coarse anecdotes.

II. i. 150 *fleet.* Properly a company of vessels sailing together, Beatrice uses the word of the company of masqueraders present. The nautical suggestion of the word leads her to continue the figure in the word *boarded,* which implies the attack of one vessel on another.

II. i. 186 *use.* It is disputed whether this word is a plain indicative or a subjunctive, equivalent to 'let all hearts . . use.' The latter seems more probable.

II. i. 196-198 *willow . . garland.* Referring to the garlands of weeping willow worn by forsaken lovers.

II. i. 207 *like the blind man,* etc. An allusion to an incident at the close of the first chapter of the Spanish novel, *Lazarillo de Tormes.*

II. i. 212 *creep into sedges.* Waterfowl, when wounded, creep for shelter into the sedges along the river bank. So Claudio will go off and pine by himself.

II. i. 217 *base though bitter.* The adjectives have been condemned as unintelligible in their context; but Benedick means to condemn the disposition of Beatrice as 'base,' *i.e.* unworthy, unjust, while admitting that her words have a sting (bitterness) which 'base' criticisms do not usually possess.

II. i. 223 *Lady Fame.* The Vergilian deity *Fama,* Rumor, who goes about the world spreading news.

II. i. 243, 244 *If their singing,* etc. 'If the birds sings as you say (*i.e.* if Hero consents to do as you intend and marry Claudio) . . . what you say is creditable to you.'

II. i. 256 *like a man at a mark.* In archery contests a man stood beside the mark to check off the contestants' arrows as they struck. It was a perilous position when the archers shot badly.

II. i. 260 *infect to the north star.* The infection of her breath would reach beyond planetary space.

II. i. 263 *made Hercules have turned spit,* etc. Beatrice would have treated Hercules worse than Omphale, who in the legend put him into domestic service. Turning the spit was the meanest office in the Elizabethan kitchen. It was often performed by dogs.

II. i. 265 *infernal Ate in good apparel.* Beatrice is like Ate, the goddess of discord, in everything except that she wears the clothes of a fashionable gentlewoman.

II. i. 266 *I would . . some scholar would conjure her.* Scholars were reputed to be able to raise up and banish evil spirits.

II. i. 278 *Prester John's foot.* Prester John was a fabled Christian king, supposed to live in some remote part of Asia or Africa.

II. i. 279 *the Great Cham's beard.* The Great Cham or Grand Khan was the ruler of the Mongols.

II. i. 280 *the Pigmies.* The fabulous race who fought with cranes.

II. i. 282 *harpy.* The Harpies were rapacious female monsters who afflicted voyagers.

II. i. 306 *civil . . civil.* A pun on civil and Seville, commonly spelled and pronounced alike. Seville oranges are bitter-sweet, neither one thing nor the other. Hence the application to Claudio. Yellow, the color of oranges, is also the color (complexion) of jealousy (l. 307).

II. i. 332 *alliance. I.e.* relationship by marriage. Beatrice teases Claudio for addressing her as 'cousin' as if he were already married to her cousin Hero.

II. i. 333 *sun-burnt.* Probably, a mild way of saying 'unattractive'; but some editors explain it as 'exposed to the sun,' unsheltered, *i.e.* a lone woman.

II. ii. 45 *term me Claudio.* Editors have found difficulty in understanding why Margaret should address Borachio by any name but his own; but how is Margaret, who is not privy to the design against her mistress, to be prevented from suspecting a plot when she hears herself loudly called 'Hero,' unless Borachio has previously persuaded her to act out a little play in which they are to simulate the happiness of the declared lovers?

II. iii. 5 *I am here already, sir.* The boy indulges in hyperbole: 'I will go so fast that you may say I am back again already.' Benedick pretends to take his words literally.

II. iii. 15 *the tabor and the pipe.* Drum and fife (l. 14) are of course the instruments of martial music; tabor (a small drum) and pipe are the corresponding instruments which appear in times of peaceful revelry.

II. iii. 35 *noble . . angel.* A pun, frequent in Shakespeare, on the names of two coins of his day. A 'noble' was worth one-third of a sovereign (*i.e.* 6s. 8d.), an 'angel' half a sovereign (10s.).

II. iii. 37 *of what colour it please God.* That is, her hair must not be dyed.

II. iii. 39, S. d. *Balthazar.* The folio edition here substitutes for 'Balthazar' the name of the actor who took his part: *Iacke Wilson.* Compare the note on IV. ii.

II. iii. 45 *kid-fox.* Since 'kid fox' does not appear to have been a current name for a young fox, many of the best editors are disposed to alter the text to 'the hid fox.'

II. iii. 49, 50 *It is the witness still of excellency,* etc. 'It is always (*still*) a proof of excellence that, in demeanour, it is unconscious, or unknowing, of its own perfection.' (Furness.)

II. iii. 59 *crotchets.* A pun on two meanings of the word: (1) whims, (2) notes of music.

II. iii. 60 *notes, notes, forsooth, and nothing!* A pun is evident here, 'nothing' being pronounced by Elizabethans much or precisely like 'noting.' It has been suggested that a similar pun is involved in the title of the play, *Much Ado about Nothing* (or *Noting, i.e.* eavesdropping).

II. iii. 90 *night-raven.* The voice of this bird (which has not been certainly identified) was supposed to betoken some 'plague,' especially sickness or death.

II. iii. 92 *Yea, marry.* These words have no reference, of course, to the speech of Benedick, who has hidden himself apart from the others (cf. l. 43). Furness explains that while Benedick speaks the Prince has been talking to Claudio about the music for Hero 'to-morrow night' (l. 94) and that he here assents to Claudio's suggestion.

II. iii. 101 *Stalk on,* etc. A figure from game-stalking. The 'fowl' is Benedick, whom they hope to catch 'sitting.'

II. iii. 261 *paper bullets of the brain.* Quips and sentences, Benedick foresees, will be shot at him like bullets, but being taken from books, they are but paper bullets, which do no real injury. For *career* in the sense of full speed, cf. V. i. 138.

III. i. 45 *as full as.* Possibly a misprint for *at full as,* 'fully as.'

III. i. 61 *spell him backward.* Alluding to the practice of conjurors, who spell prayers and holy names backwards in order to produce incantations. The meaning is: turn his virtues into vices.

III. i. 101 *every day—to-morrow.* The meaning seems to be: 'I am married every day—it is constantly in my thoughts; but the actual time is to-morrow.' Perhaps, however, Hero refers to the postponement of the ceremony (cf. II. i. 374 ff.) and means: 'Every day it is set for the next.'

III. i. 110 *behind the back. I.e.* when their back is turned, when people talk about them.

III. i. 112 *Taming my wild heart to thy loving hand.* A figure suggested by the taming of a hawk, which comes to know the hand of the falconer.

III. ii. 24 *hang . . draw.* Alluding to the punishment of traitors, who were hanged, drawn, and quartered.

III. ii. 27 *a humour or a worm.* Contemporary dental theory ascribed toothache, among other causes, to the presence of humors, *i.e.* unhealthy secretions, and to actual worms in the teeth.

III. ii. 37 *no doublet.* That is, no doublet is to be seen, because, like a Spaniard, the upper part of his body is quite enveloped by his cloak.

III. ii. 46, 47 *the old ornament of his cheek hath already stuffed tennis-balls.* He has cut off his beard. The tennis-balls of the day were sometimes stuffed with human hair.

III. ii. 70 *buried with her face upwards.* Suicides were sometimes buried with their faces downward. The Prince means that Beatrice will not be responsible for her own death.

III. ii. 75 *hobby-horses.* Originally morris-dancers dressed to look like horses; hence any ridiculously frivolous persons.

III. ii. 90 This line should perhaps be assigned to Claudio.

III. iii. 106 *scab.* Modern usage of 'scab' for a scurvy fellow renders the pun still intelligible.

III. iii. 143 *god Bel's priests.* Threescore and ten priests of Bel are mentioned in the Apocryphal book of *Daniel.*

III. iii. 147 *the fashion wears out more apparel than the man.* That is, new clothes are required oftener to conform to changes of fashion than for actual use.

III. iii. 176 *right Master constable.* An absurd title. The speaker is thinking of such respectful phrases as 'right worshipful.'

III. iii. 188, 189 *commodity . . bills.* 'Bills'

is used punningly with reference, first to the bills (halberds) of the watch; second, to the common commercial phrase, 'to take up a commodity on one's bills,' *i.e.* buy merchandise on credit.

III. iv. 13 *within.* Furness prefers to take 'tire within' as meaning the inner trimming of the head dress. *Within* may, however, mean 'in an inner room.'

III. iv. 32 *saving your reverence.* A common expression, sometimes abbreviated 'sir-reverence.' It means that no disrespect to the hearer is intended.

III. v. 18 *palabras.* A scrap of Spanish: *pocas palabras,* few words.

III. v. 37 *when the age is in,* etc. An original adaptation of an old proverb: 'When ale is in, wit is out.'

III. v. 39 *God's a good man.* A proverbial saying.

III. v. 68 *non-come.* Dogberry probably means 'non plus,' but confuses that bit of learning with another: 'non compos mentis.'

IV. i. 22 *some be of laughing, as ah! ha! he!* Alluding to the way Latin and English grammars of the day listed the interjections according to the emotions they expressed.

IV. i. 45 *in your own proof.* 'In making trial of her yourself.' (Wright.)

IV. i. 69 *True!* Hero's exclamation refers to Don John's speech, not Benedick's.

IV. i. 83 *Hero itself,* etc. 'The very name, by becoming a byword and a reproach, can blot out virtue.' (Furness.)

IV. i. 140 *That I myself was to myself not mine.* *I.e.* Hero was so much a part of me that by comparison I was not myself.

IV. i. 169 *The tenour of my book.* 'Book' is used in the general sense of the learning gained from books, the tenor or general nature of which is warranted (*i.e.* confirmed) by the Friar's practical observations of life.

IV. i. 239 *But if all aim but this be levell'd false.* 'If every other aim miscarry.'

IV. i. 254 *For to strange sores strangely they strain the cure.* 'Strange diseases require desperately strange cures.'

IV. ii. The early editions, both quarto and folio, prefix to the speeches of Dogberry and Verges in this scene the names of the actors who originally took their parts; *viz.*, Kempe and Cowley respectively. The phrase 'in gowns' in the opening stage direction means that the constables and town clerk (sexton) wore their gowns of office.

IV. ii. 5 *Dogb.* In this case the early editions give the speech to 'Andrew,' perhaps a nickname of the clown or Merry-Andrew, Kempe.

IV. ii. 73, 74. In the early editions these lines form a single speech, printed thus: 'Let them be in the hands of Coxcombe.' The folio gives the words to the Sexton, the quarto to Cowley (*i.e.* Verges). Malone suggested the accepted reading, which cannot be regarded as certain.

V. i. 16 *Bid sorrow wag.* Capell's emendation. The early editions have 'And sorrow, wagge,' which apparently makes no sense.

V. i. 38 *made a push.* The most probable meaning is made a 'pish!', *i.e.* mocked.

V. i. 82 *Win me and wear me.* A proverbial phrase: 'He may have me if he wins me (by the sword).'

V. i. 102 *wake your patience.* 'We will not keep your patience wakeful or excited.' It would be more natural to say 'wake your impatience,' but the Prince is too polite to use the uncomplimentary term.

V. i. 131 *draw.* The word is used punningly, with special reference to bidding the minstrels draw their bows across the strings of their instruments.

V. i. 142 *broke cross.* Like 'in the career' above (l. 138), this is a figure from the tilting matches of the day. Only a very awkward tilter would aim so badly as to break his staff 'cross,' *i.e.* not by a direct blow, but by allowing it to strike lengthwise across his opponent's body.

V. i. 146 *turn his girdle.* A common proverbial saying of rather vague force. Probably it means no more than 'change his mood,' but it has also been explained as 'prepare to fight,' referring to the alleged custom of wrestlers to turn the buckles of their girdles to the back before beginning.

V. i. 170 *a wise gentleman.* Evidently the words, as repeated by Beatrice, had some colloquial derogatory force now lost. Perhaps they were a cant name for a fool.

V. i. 208, 209 *goes in his doublet and hose and leaves off his wit.* Doublet and hose formed the Elizabethan undress costume, a cloak being worn over them on formal occasions. The Prince suggests ironically that man's wit is a mere outward embellishment which he can leave off as easily as he can his cloak and go about in his natural stupidity.

V. i. 210 *He is then a giant to an ape,* etc. In physical proportions man is much greater than an ape (*i.e.* an Elizabethan pet ape, a small monkey), but in mental power the ape is far superior.

V. i. 235 *one meaning well suited.* One meaning provided with many different suits of clothes; alluding to the previous speech of Don Pedro, where practically the same idea is expressed in four different ways.

V. i. 334 *God save the foundation.* A customary phrase, used by those who received assistance from a charitable foundation, quite out of place here since Leonato is not a 'foundation.'

V. ii. 6 *so high a style.* A pun on the two words, 'style' and 'stile,' is intended; 'come over' in the next line implying both 'excel' the style and 'climb over' the stile.

V. ii. 21 *with a vice.* A play on 'vice,' the screw by which the sharp pointed 'pike' was fastened in the centre of the buckler, and 'vice,' sin.

V. ii. 30, 31 *Leander . . Troilus.* Allusions probably to Marlowe's *Hero and Leander* and Chaucer's *Troilus and Criseide* respectively.

V. ii. 41 *not born under a riming planet.* Alluding to the old-fashioned belief in the influence exerted upon each man's temperament by the particular planet which was most conspicuous when he was born.

V. ii. 82 *in the time of good neighbours.* In the time when people's neighbours used to speak well of them—a very long time ago.

V. ii. 89 *Don Worm, his conscience.* The old moralists represented conscience as a gnawing worm. The title 'Don' is given it from mock respect.

V. iii. 9, 10 *Hang thou there upon the tomb,* etc. Dr. Furness holds that these lines are not Claudio's comment while affixing the epitaph, but part of the epitaph itself; but compare Claudio's similar riming comment below, ll. 22, 23.

V. iii. 20 *Till death be uttered.* There has been much unnecessary discussion of the meaning of this passage. It is clear if we understand *uttered* in the common Elizabethan sense of 'sent abroad,' 'put into circulation.' The word is regularly so used with regard to books placed on sale, news made public, etc. The meaning here is, then, that the graves are to yawn and yield their dead until death is scattered abroad among the world of men.

V. iii. 33 *Than this,* etc. 'This' probably refers to Hero: 'May Hymen grant us a happier outcome than he granted to her whose marriage was the means of her death.' Hymen is the god of marriage. Dr. Furness explains 'Than this' as a contraction for 'than in this (issue).'

V. iv. 6 *In the true course of all the question.* 'Now that the whole question has been truly followed up.'

V. iv. 43 *I think he thinks upon the savage bull.* A jesting reminiscence of the conversation between Don Pedro and Benedick, I. i. 270-278.

V. iv. 45, 46 *Europa . . Europa.* In the first instance the continent of Europe, in the second the mythological maiden, supposed to have been carried off by Jupiter in the form of a bull, and to have given her name to the land whither she was brought.

V. iv. 70 *let wonder seem familiar.* 'Act as if your curiosity had already been satisfied.'

V. iv. 99, 100 *'Benedick, the married man.'* See I. i. 278.

V. iv. 104 *beaten with brains.* Subjected to ridicule. If a man fears ridicule, Benedick says, he will not dare to have anything handsome about him (whether clothes or a wife), which might attract attention to him.

V. iv. 116 *a double-dealer.* Used punningly, first of one who gives up his single life for the double life of matrimony, and then with an allusion to double-dealing, inconstancy.

APPENDIX A

Sources of 'Much Ado about Nothing'

Much Ado about Nothing is a good example of the sort of originality which usually marks Shakespeare's plots. No source other than the poet's own invention has been discovered for those parts of the play which give it its particular charm and interest—the story of Benedick and Beatrice and the delectable folly of Dogberry. The famous scenes constructed about these figures seem to be based solely upon Shakespeare's knowledge of contemporary English character, as he had studied it in cultivated and in plebeian circles respectively. The author turned to books for his material only in the case of the story of Hero and Claudio.

The tale of two lovers, estranged by an envious villain by means of a sham interview between the lady and another man, has been found in the literature of many countries. It is likely that Shakespeare knew it in the form developed by the Italian story-writer, Matteo Bandello (1480-1561), the twentieth tale of whose collection (published at Lucca in 1554) 'telleth how Signor Timbreo di Cardona (Shakespeare's Claudio) being with King Piero of Arragon (Shakespeare's Don Pedro) in Messina, became enamoured of Fenicia Lionata (Shakespeare's Hero, daughter of Leonato), and of the various and unlooked-for chances which befell before he took her to wife.'

In this story we have the same scene of action as in Shakespeare and the same general progress of events, though there are important differences of detail. The names, except Don Pedro and Leonato, are quite unlike. The deception of the lover in Bandello is achieved simply by showing him a man entering a window of Leonato's house; there is no parallel to the disguising of Margaret to simulate her mistress. Again, in Bandello, the denunciation of the heroine is performed less dramatically and also less heartlessly than in Shakespeare, by means of a messenger sent by the deceived lover to her father's house; and the villain himself exposes his plot from subsequent scruples of conscience. Thus Bandello's representatives of both Claudio and Don John are shown in a less odious light than their Shakespearean counterparts. Bandello appears to regard them both as rather excellent young men; Shakespeare, with distinctly different ideals of conduct, is at pains to emphasize his disapproval.

It would hardly be doubted that Shakespeare had read Bandello, if we were certain that he could read Italian. Probably he could, since Italian was the most commonly studied of all the modern tongues in his age and was perhaps more generally understood by educated men than any foreign language is in England to-day. No English translation of Bandello's tale is known to have existed in Shakespeare's lifetime, but a free French version, by François de Belle-Forest, was published in 1582. This may possibly have furnished the poet with the story, but the likelihood that it did so is lessened by the fact that Shakespeare shows no acquaintance with any of Belle-Forest's rather numerous deviations from his original. Another possibility is that Shakespeare knew Bandello's story at second hand, as it had been worked up into some earlier English play. Evidence for such a drama has been found in a record of the Revels Accounts for December 18, 1574, which shows that the Earl of Leicester's players acted a piece called 'theier matter of Panecia' (*i.e.* Phenicia or Fenicia, Bandello's heroine?), when Shakespeare was ten years old.

For one of Shakespeare's divergences from Bandello noted above—the introduction of Margaret in Hero's clothes—a source exists in Ariosto's *Orlando Furioso,* Book V (published, 1516), where a story somewhat similar to Bandello's is related. In all other details Ariosto's version is far less like *Much Ado* than Bandello's, but the former clearly foreshadows the part of Margaret in his Dalinda, whom he makes the narrator of the tale. In the fourth canto of the second book of the *Fairy Queen* (published, 1590), Spenser introduces an adaptation of Ariosto's story, again changing the names and putting the narrative into the mouth of the figure corresponding to Claudio. Thus the latter portrays his sentiments while the deception is being practiced upon him:

Eftsoones he came vnto th' appointed place,
And with him brought *Pryene* [Margaret], rich arayd,
In *Claribellaes* [Hero's] clothes. Her proper face
I not descerned in that darkesome shade,
But weend it was my loue, with whom he playd.
Ah God, what horrour and tormenting griefe
My hart, my hands, mine eyes, and all assayd?
Me liefer were ten thousand deathes priefe [experience]
Then wound of gealous worme, and shame of such repriefe.

The figures of Dogberry and his companions and their whole connection with the plot were original with Shakespeare, as has been said. How truly the poet depicted the actual constabulary of his time is proved by a genuine letter written August 10, 1586, by Lord Burghley, Queen Elizabeth's chief minister of state, to Sir Francis Walsingham:

'Sir—As I cam from London homward, in my coche, I sawe at euery townes end the nombre of x. or xij. standyng, with long staues, and vntill I cam to Enfield I thought no other of them, but that they had stayd for auoyding of the rayne, or to drynk at some alehouses, for so they did stand vnder pentyces [penthouses] at alehouses. But at Enfeld fynding a dosen in a plump [group], whan ther was no rayne, I bethought myself that they war apoynted as watchmen, for the apprehendyng of such as ar missyng [*i.e.* certain escaped traitors]; and thereuppon I called some of them to me apart, and asked them wherfor they stood ther? and on of them answered,—To tak 3 yong men. And demandyng how they shuld know the persons, on answered with these words:—Mary, my Lord, by intelligence of ther fauor. What meane you by that? quoth I. Marry, sayd they, on of the partyes hath a hooked nose.—And haue you, quoth I, no other mark?—No, sayth they. And then I asked who apoynted them; and they answered on Bankes, a Head Constable, whom I willed to be sent to me.—Suerly, sir, who so euer had the chardg from yow hath vsed the matter negligently, for these watchmen stand so oppenly in plumps, as no suspected person will come neare them; and if they be no better instructed but to fynd 3 persons by on of them hauyng a hooked nose, they may miss therof. And thus I thought good to aduertise yow, that the Justyces that had the chardg, as I thynk, may vse the matter more circumspectly.'

APPENDIX B

The History of the Play

The definite history of *Much Ado about Nothing* goes back to the first year of the seventeenth century. On August 23, 1600, this play was licensed for publication, along with the second part of *Henry IV*, and it appeared in the same year in the only early quarto edition. This version was evidently followed by the publishers of the collected edition of Shakespeare's plays in the 1623 Folio, and the two texts exhibit only trivial differences. It is generally assumed that the comedy was written in 1599, and there is no reason for inferring an earlier date, except the bare possibility that *Much Ado about Nothing* is identical with a mysterious *Love's Labor's Won*, listed by Francis Meres as one of Shakespeare's comedies in 1598.

The title-page of the edition of 1600 records that the play 'hath been sundrie times publikely acted by the right honorable, the Lord Chamberlaine his seruants,' *i.e.* by Shakespeare's company, then acting at the newly built Globe Theatre. A memorandum in the Stationers' Register, dated August 4 (1600), less than three weeks before the official license for publication, notes that *Much Ado about Nothing* and three other plays performed by Shakespeare's company were 'to be staied,' *i.e.* withheld from publication. The purpose of this unsuccessful effort to prevent the printing of the comedy was doubtless the actors' fear that circulation of the printed text might detract from the success of their performances. The substitution in the early editions of the names of Jack Wilson, Kempe and Cowley instead of Balthazar, Dogberry and Verges (*cf.* notes on II. iii. 39, *s. d.* and IV. ii.) gives welcome information regarding the creators of those parts.

Much Ado about Nothing was acted at Court, probably twice, on the occasion of the marriage of James I's daughter, the Princess Elizabeth, to Frederic, Elector Palatine, in 1613. More specific evidence of the play's popularity with Stuart audiences occurs in a poem by Leonard Digges, affixed to the 1640 edition of Shakespeare's *Poems:*

> Let but *Beatrice*
> And *Benedicke* be seene, loe, in a trice
> The Cockpit, Galleries, Boxes, all are full.

After the Restoration, Sir William Davenant (1606-1668) was responsible for an ill-advised effort to make capital out of Benedick and Beatrice by introducing them into the plot of Shakespeare's *Measure for Measure,* in a medley called *The Law against Lovers* (published, 1673). A further monstrosity appeared in 1736 in *The Universal Passion,* an attempt by one James Miller to combine *Much Ado* with Molière's *Princess of Elis.* In 1721, the genuine play was restored to the London stage, where it has since been an established favorite. David Garrick (1717-1779) was famous in the rôle of Benedick, as a great many of the chief English and American actors have been since. In general, however, the impersonators of Beatrice have found the greatest opportunity, and distinguished actresses like Helena Faucit (Lady Martin, 1817-1898), Ellen Terry (1848-——), and Ada Rehan (1860-1916) have owed much of their success to their interpretations of this part.

APPENDIX C

Suggestions for Collateral Reading

William Hazlitt in *Characters of Shakespear's Plays* (1817). (Reprinted in Everyman's Library.)

Mrs. Anna Jameson in *Characteristics of Women, Moral, Poetical and Historical* (1833).

Mary Cowden Clarke: 'Beatrice and Hero: The Cousins' in *The Girlhood of Shakespeare's Heroines* (1850-1852). (In vol. iii of the Everyman's Library ed.)

Helena Faucit, Lady Martin: *On Some of Shakespeare's Female Characters,* Letter no. viii. 'Beatrice' (1885). Seventh ed., Edinburgh, 1904.

Andrew Lang: *The Comedies of Shakespeare.* With Illustrations by E. A. Abbey, and comments by Andrew Lang. V. *Much Ado about Nothing.* Harper's Magazine, September, 1891, vol. lxxxiii, pp. 489-502.

H. H. Furness: *A New Variorum Edition of Shakespeare.* Vol. xii. *Much Ado about Nothing,* 1899.

APPENDIX D

The Text of the Present Edition

The text of the present volume is, by permission of the Oxford University Press, that of the Oxford Shakespeare, edited by the late W. J. Craig, except for the following deviations:

1. The stage directions are based on those in the two original editions of the play, a few obvious errors in the latter being corrected and words there missing added within square brackets.

2. About half a dozen words are differently spelled: *e.g.*, antic (antick), lantern (lanthorn), villainy (villany), haggard (haggerd).

3. Five changes of punctuation or wording have been made, viz.:

I. i. 153 Leonato.— *for* Leonato:
II. iii. 92 marry. Dost *for* marry; dost
II. iii. 123 sit you— *for* sit you;
III. i. 101 day— *for* day,
V. i. 94 Scambling *for* Scrambling

INDEX OF WORDS GLOSSED

(Figures in full-faced type refer to page-numbers)